"I've learn

He shifted or
hers, and a n... ...skittered along her limbs. "Like the way your drawl gets heavy and that cool exterior slips when you're angry." His gaze traveled across her face, and the transformation to lazy charm was instantaneous. "It also happens when you're fighting the attraction between us."

Her heart tripped before picking up speed.

With a hard swallow, she refused to look away. Because that would be admitting he was right. And as she met his gaze, she could feel the old awareness rise from the ashes like a phoenix.

"I think you're confusing irritation with attraction," she said, shooting for a lofty, confident air, but knowing she fell horribly short.

His eyes went dark. "Am I?" he said as he swept the hair from her face, his fingers lingering on her cheek.

A shower of shivers coursed down her spine, and the resulting blaze melted the tension in her back and muddled her brain. She was vaguely aware ice cream dripped onto her fingers. But the cold droplets did little to extinguish the heat in her body. She sat, paralyzed, as his eyes dropped to her lips, increasing her internal Fahrenheit reading to the boiling point.

"A challenge like that is impossible to resist," he murmured.

AIMEE CARSON The summer she turned eleven, Aimee left the children's section of the library and entered an aisle full of Mills & Boon® novels. She promptly pulled out a book, sat on the floor and read the entire story. It has been a love affair that has lasted for more than thirty years.

Despite a fantastic job working part-time as a physician in the Alaskan bush (think *Northern Exposure and E.R.,* minus the beautiful mountains and George Clooney), she also enjoys being at home in the gorgeous Black Hills of South Dakota, riding her dirt bike with her three wonderful kids and her beyond-patient husband. But, whether at home or at work, every morning is spent creating the stories she loves so much.

Her motto? Life is too short to do anything less than what you absolutely love. She counts herself lucky to have two jobs she adores and incredibly blessed to be a part of Mills & Boon's family of talented authors.

This is Aimee Carson's first book for Harlequin Presents EXTRA!

SECRET HISTORY OF A GOOD GIRL

AIMEE CARSON

~ Unbuttoned by a Rebel~

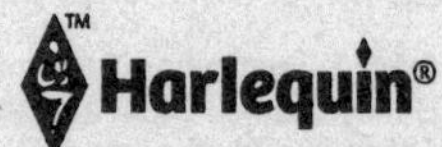

TORONTO NEW YORK LONDON
AMSTERDAM PARIS SYDNEY HAMBURG
STOCKHOLM ATHENS TOKYO MILAN MADRID
PRAGUE WARSAW BUDAPEST AUCKLAND

Recycling programs for this product may not exist in your area.

ISBN-13: 978-0-373-52856-1

SECRET HISTORY OF A GOOD GIRL

First North American Publication 2012

This edition published by arrangement with Harlequin Books S.A.

For questions and comments about the quality of this book please contact us at Customer_eCare@Harlequin.ca.

www.Harlequin.com

Printed in U.S.A.

Dear Reader,

Reading a book by a new author is a bit like going on a blind date—awkward in the beginning, but ripe with possibility and the anticipation of the unknown. So, dear reader, in celebration of my debut novel I'd like to ease this first-meeting awkwardness by sharing my favorite recipe for the perfect romance:

AIMEE'S FAVORITE, MELT-IN-YOUR-HEART ROMANCE RECIPE

1 heroine—handpicked for her sassy attitude, quirky imperfections and ability to laugh at herself; virginity is optional

1 hero—selected for his hotness, audacious charm and sprinkling of faults; sense of humor a must—see sassiness of heroine above

dash of personal growth and gut-wrenching emotional truthiness

pinch of conflict

toss in a few surprises and a generous helping of FUN

Stir until ingredients are combined, the fun is evenly distributed and lumps of faults and imperfections are of a tolerable size. Bake, let cool and frost with your favorite setting. My choice was easy. Although the various hotels, clubs and restaurants mentioned in my book are fictitious, South Miami Beach's Ocean Drive and the sparkling Atlantic are very much real.

To my kids.

CHAPTER ONE

WELL, this was it. She'd come full circle. Back to where her dream of organizing glamorous events had been born and was now about to be realized. If she could get the job, that was.

But first she had to conquer her lame phobia of gilded front doors.

Alyssa Hunt stared across South Miami Beach's Ocean Avenue at the Samba Hotel. As part of the renovations, workmen in overalls applied touch-up paint around the arched windows, the afternoon sun glinting off the glass. A salty Atlantic breeze rustled the fuchsia-tipped hibiscus lining the path to the staff entrance in back.

Years ago, she'd donned her waitress uniform to work at least a dozen catering jobs at the luxury hotel. And always, *always* entered via the rear.

She tugged on the jacket of her off-the-rack gray suit, shifting her gaze from the ornate front entry to the walkway that led to the service entrance. No mocking doorways back there.

With a frown, she let out a soft sigh of exasperation and gripped the handle of her tote.

Come on, Alyssa. Quit being such a wuss. It's time to take your business to the next level. And hovering in a quasi-purgatory state of indecision won't get you what you want.

She took a deep breath and waited for a break between cars. When it came, she crossed the road, boldly striding for the front door.

Fifteen minutes later Alyssa exited the elevator into the bright sunshine of the Samba's rooftop deck, heading toward a row of chaise longues. She was too stunned to take in the scenery. And as the realization she was one step closer to success finally sank in, she stopped to set her tote down and clutch the back of a chair, pressing a hand over her eyes.

"Are you all right?"

The deep baritone voice echoed across the water of the pool, but Alyssa ignored the interloper.

Of course she was all right. She'd shown up. She'd conquered her ludicrous fear of fancy entryways. Best of all, she'd scored an appointment for an interview. For a gig she wasn't quite qualified for. Oh, she could do the job. She knew she could. It was exactly the kind of contract she'd been preparing for since she started Elite Events. Unfortunately, now she had to convince the owner. Not the manager, the *owner*.

Her stomach rolled, and she dropped her palm to her belly, as if she could soothe the jittery butterflies engaged in a feeding frenzy over her nerves.

"Lady, maybe you should take a seat before you keel over."

The voice was followed by a rhythmic splash of water. Whoever it was, he was swimming in her direction. And though she wasn't about to keel over, thank you very much, maybe his advice was sound.

Besides, she'd hate to find out she was wrong and ruin her skirt.

She rounded the chair, dropping into the cushioned seat. Elbows on her thighs, forehead against her fingers, she stared down at her feet and blew out a breath.

So what if none of the events on her résumé were as grand

as those at a five-star hotel? So what if she'd chosen safer—albeit less exciting—small corporate events? She'd learned a lot since she started her business. And she was good. She *knew* she was good.

Arrange a kickass employee appreciation party on a budget? No problem. Keep her cool at a retirement luncheon as the intoxicated retiree barfed on her shoes? Bring it on.

But *jeez…*

Ten years after her royal screw-up, and five years after starting her business, she was finally applying for a job that catered to the moneyed set. A class of society responsible for countless humiliating memories. It had taken her all night to psyche herself up to ask for a meeting with the manager. And now she had to face the billionaire owner, Paulo Domingues.

Billionaire. With a boldfaced capital *B*.

Her stomach flipped again, and she closed her eyes, using deep breathing exercises to regain control. Which went well until sparkles of light began to shimmer behind her eyelids. It took a moment for her to realize she was teetering on the edge of hyperventilation.

Clearly her relaxation technique sucked.

"Here," the man said from beyond the twinkling darkness. "Take this."

She forced herself to inhale slowly, lifted her lids, and caught sight of her high-heeled sandals—the token designer accessory she'd added for a hint of style. Oh, good, no more annoying sparklies in her peripheral vision. With her breathing finally in line, she shifted her attention forward and spied bare masculine feet, water pooling on the deck around them.

Her gaze slid up past a pair of muscular thighs. With a growing sense of unease, she moved on to lean hips enveloped in a Speedo and then a flat abdomen. This was followed by an underwear model chest, complete with the obligatory ripples.

Sunshine glinted off rivulets coursing down the sculpted torso as the man held out a bottle of water in her direction.

Alyssa was handling the disturbing image just fine until he gave a shake of his black hair—and flying water droplets landed close to her pricey high heels.

With a faint disgusted sound she leaned over to check the leather. She'd paid a mint for those shoes. She lifted her head, preparing to give the man hell…

Until her gaze met his. Dark eyes. With a hint of heat. Eyes housed in the handsome face of Paulo Domingues. Her mouth froze, and her blood drained lower, her head growing light.

Great. What sick, twisted turn of karmic fate was this?

He continued to hold out the bottle, his forehead creased with concern. "You look pale."

Uh…yeah. Because all her blood had reconvened south of her belly button.

Like many in this city, his muted Latino heritage was tinctured with an American flavor that matched his accent. But just because she'd been presented with a vista of downtown Miami to the west, cerulean sky over the Atlantic to the east, and a shimmering pool garnished with a fantasy-worthy, ridiculously wealthy male specimen, she was not going to swoon.

She *never* swooned. Damnit, she was better than that.

He nodded at the bottle in his hand. "Drink this." A sexy half-smile flickered across his face. "And then I'll get you something stronger."

There wasn't enough alcohol in the world to get her through the next few minutes.

Her heart thrummed beneath her ribs, and she accepted the offer with a nod of thanks.

As she sipped the icy water, her gaze followed him anxiously as he crossed to a table piled with clothes and swiped a towel down his legs. He pulled on jeans over his bathing suit, and she relaxed in relief. But then he returned to stand in front of her, folding his bicep-laden arms across his beautifully naked chest, scanning her face as if to assess if she was okay.

The concern was nice, but for crying out loud, what was with the shirtless Taylor Lautner impression? And why couldn't she finish her panic attack in peace?

Hoping he'd take the hint, she checked her watch and then looked up at him, searching for a gracious way to tell him to take a hike. And, please God, don't let her hick accent surface. "I believe we have an appointment in fifteen minutes."

His eyes lit with a twinkle. "Nice to know you can speak." He headed for a nearby corner bar, bypassing the table with his remaining clothes. "Otherwise it would have been a very short interview, Ms....?"

Shoot, he was *still* bare-chested. "Alyssa Hunt."

"So, Ms. Hunt," he said as he pulled out a soda and raised it in offering. "Would you like some caffeinated sugar?"

Really? That was his idea of something stronger? Alyssa simply declined with a shake of her head.

"It might help you prepare for the interview," he went on.

Prepare. Well, there was an idea. Last evening, when she'd heard about the sudden opening at the Samba, she'd learned as much as she could about his property. A shining star regarded as the industry's hippest new hotel. But there was no time to read about the owner. Other than his rebel image, aided by his shocking departure from his family's mega resort chain, she didn't know much. And she never went in so blind about a client.

"I'll admit the short notice left little time for research," she said.

"My event planner's departure yesterday took me by surprise, too." His half-grin turned into a full, complete with dimples. "So, just to be fair, I'll give you ten minutes to pump me for information."

With a little grimace, she wrinkled her nose delicately. At

least she hoped it was delicate. "That sounds so harsh. I prefer the phrase..." She searched for a more acceptable term. "Tactical reconnaissance."

His brows rose. "Are you preparing for an interview or a combat mission?"

Confident her professional air had finally returned, she stood, smoothing a hand down her jacket. The concrete and steel forest of downtown Miami gleamed in the distance beyond him. "You can always hope for the former," she said coolly. "But it's best to prepare for the latter."

A glint of awareness appeared in his eyes. "Should I be afraid?"

His suggestive tone set her on guard, but she held his gaze, refusing to play. The bad boy image was all well and good, but she had no time for games. "I doubt you scare so easily, Mr. Domingues."

As his lips twitched, she braced for his reply. But when it came, it was without his previous undertones. "What would you like to know about me?"

She hesitated. Anything she said was likely to reveal more about her than him, and the male expanse of chest was most troubling. But the opportunity was too good to pass.

Alyssa picked up her bag and crossed the teak deck, sitting on the barstool across from him. "What do you think I should ask?" she said with a polite smile.

Obviously tickled by her reply, he braced a hand against the counter. "You're going to make me do all the work?" She lifted a noncommittal shoulder, and he pursed his lips. "Okay. I would want to know if I'm dealing with a straight-shooter or someone who beats around the bush." Alyssa tipped her head in question, and he answered, "Straight-shooter."

The roguish look returned to his face. "On the other hand..." His eyes boldly swept down to her waist and back, triggering a barrage of disconcerting sensations in her body. "You should ask if you'll have my undivided attention or if my gaze will repeatedly drift to your legs."

Ignoring the hammering in her chest, she resisted the urge to roll her eyes and folded her hands on the counter. Her tone was careful. "Fascinating. That isn't a question I would have considered."

"You would have considered it." A grin flashed. "You just wouldn't have asked it."

True. And she always appreciated blunt honesty. "And the answer is…?"

His dimples grew deeper. "Yes to both."

Cocky little charmer. While most people were working hard for their pay, here he was swimming in the middle of the day, but his easygoing nature was hard to resist. "I appreciate the warning." She hiked a brow drolly. "Should I be aware of any other chauvinistic character traits?"

"Oh, I'm much more subtle than that."

Ha. There was nothing subtle about him. Neither his confidence nor his to-die-for looks nor his bazillion-dollar smile. Feeling the need for a shield, she folded her arms across her chest. "So exactly how hard a sell are you during a job interview?"

He parked his elbows on the counter, bringing his face level with hers, his eyes flickering with an unmistakable light. "Depends on the bait."

Bait? She blinked. Whatever allure she held, it was nothing compared to his thick eyelashes. The chin-length black hair brushed back from flawless skin. Or the dark slash of eyebrows that added a rugged touch and contrasted nicely against full lips.

She leaned back to gain some distance and crossed her legs. And while she sensed his teasing was all in fun, it was best he learned Alyssa Hunt didn't take crap from anybody anymore.

She sent him her well-perfected I-won't-be-tempted smile. "I don't dangle myself in front of anyone, Mr. Domingues."

The man tipped back his head and laughed. Deep. Rich. Radiating humor to its very core. The kind that wrapped around you, encouraging you to join in no matter what your troubles. And he was clearly trouble.

When his chuckle finally died out, he said, "Sure we can't continue this over a drink?" His gaze turned positively wicked. "A mojito, perhaps?"

Alyssa's body froze. During her luncheon for the Hot Bods Agency, with every hunky Miami model in attendance, she'd been hit on repeatedly. And she'd had no problem dealing with the six-pack of tall, dark and handsomes at her table. Surely she could handle just one?

Her lips twisted dryly. "I think I've learned enough." And then some. "Perhaps, since you were so kind, I should return the favor?"

"Lady." His face filled with skeptical humor. "I don't need to pump you for information."

Pow. He really knew how to hit where it hurt. He was the rich hotelier and she was the peon with a rinky-dink business.

Alyssa bit her tongue, holding back the snarky retort. Wealthy charmer or not, he stood between her and her dream account, so she forced the pleasant expression to remain on her face.

"But I suppose a few questions wouldn't hurt," he went on. "Where did you work last?"

"Actually—" pride crept into her voice "—I have my own event planning business."

"Freelance?"

Heck yeah, because she'd worked her tail off since she was fifteen, occasionally getting treated like a lowly servant by the guests. But that was okay. She appreciated the valuable lesson. The only orders she'd ever take again were from her clients.

She lifted her chin. "I prefer to be the boss."

"Me, too." The glimmer in his eyes returned. "Doesn't bode well for us, now does it?" What did he mean by that? While she dealt with the confusion at his words, he continued. "And I'm looking for an in-house planner."

Maintaining his gaze, she ignored the deficiencies in her résumé and focused on the accomplishments. "I think if you listen to my pitch you'll change your mind."

The amusement returned full force. "You think so, huh?" His mesmerizing eyes held hers as he rounded the bar to lean his wonderfully muscled swimmer's frame against the counter.

Suddenly, she *did* regret refusing a drink. And forget the fruity mojito. She needed a shot of whiskey. Because the man looked very comfortable in his skin…all that wonderfully exposed tan skin drying in the sun. The urge to drop her eyes to his chest was strong, but she steadfastly held his gaze. Looking down would be sensual suicide.

After a pause, he finally went on. "Don't you have an interview soon?" He raised his eyebrows meaningfully. "Wouldn't want to be late." He cocked his head, eyes sparkling with humor. "First impressions are important."

She pressed her lips together, holding back the laugh. Oh, he was smooth. Very smooth. But she had the sale of the century to pull off, so she sent him her best self-assured smile. "That's right," she said, and inwardly cringed at her twangy words. After years of practice, the country accent still couldn't be totally contained. "So, if you'll excuse me." She slid off her seat and picked up her tote, lifting what she hoped was a dignified brow. "I have a job to land." And with a confidence she didn't feel, she turned and walked toward the exit. Other than the clap of her heels, silence followed until she was five feet from the elevator doors.

"Good luck with your pitch," he said, his voice sounding amused again.

Paulo watched the lady walk away with a regal air, hips swaying gracefully.

Outrageous. Abso-freakin'-lutely outrageous.

The combination of professional businesswoman and spunky attitude was riveting. The fitted skirt hugged a shapely backside and extended to her knees, her spectacular shoes the only style in a painfully bland outfit. With a push of a button, the swish of the elevator door, she disappeared behind a curtain of stainless steel, and his body slowly began to unwind from the knot it was cinched into.

After spending a hot morning outside, conferring with the landscaper, he'd needed a dip in the pool before checking the contractor's work in the penthouse. And now his instincts—instincts that never failed—hadn't been able to determine if Ms. Alyssa Hunt shared in the attraction or not. But *he* needed a shower. Maybe two. And most definitely cold.

He also needed to get his head out of the gutter.

But ten minutes later Paulo decided frigid showers were overrated in their ability to quash an attack of lust. His certainly hadn't helped. After pulling on clean clothes, he left the room he'd kept for his personal use during the renovations still preoccupied with thoughts of Alyssa Hunt. His mind was filled to the brim with a delicious picture of her, and Paulo's slow simmer kept returning to a rolling boil.

Smoky eyes. Delicate features. Her look had screamed professional. But the sharp tongue—tinged with an intermittent drawl—hinted at the possibility for passion beneath. And the killer body couldn't be disguised by the uptight business suit.

As he turned down the hallway leading to his office, anticipation coiled around his libido and his body tightened in response.

Paulo paused in his doorway, taking a moment to enjoy the sight of the woman in the chair across from his mahogany desk. Honey-colored hair fell in a sleek line to her shoulders, and she sat with a dainty precision. Back straight. Legs crossed. Hands folded on her lap.

When their eyes met, he felt a current of awareness, and he held her gaze as he crossed the floor. He'd give anything to see her sassy side return. "Before we get started, would you like to ask me any more questions?"

The cool gray eyes didn't flicker. But the luscious strawberry-colored lips sent him a genteel smile. "I'd prefer to explain why I'm the answer to your event planner problem."

He leaned back against the front of his desk. He had a problem, all right. Several of them.

After the smooth purchase and renovation of the Samba, now everything was falling apart. The event planner had deserted him. His general manager had left to deal with an emergency at another one of Paulo's hotels. And, to top it off, the band scheduled for the grand opening had reneged on their contract.

Typical. It *would* happen when the most important opening of his career was just eighteen days away. He'd waited years to prove Marcos wrong about the Samba.

With a small frown, he pushed the thoughts of his brother aside. "I hope you can help me too," he said. "But I need to learn a lot more about you first."

Desperation flit across her heart-shaped face before it went blank. What was the flash of panic for?

As soon as the thought formed, he squashed it. Her vulnerabilities had nothing to do with him. Whether or not he hired her would be based on her abilities.

After half a decade of killing himself at Domingues International, Paulo had finally wised up and broken free to carve out his own business vision, in his own way. No more sacrificing his life on the altar of success for a family who never noticed. No more following the Domingues creed of eating, sleeping and breathing the job, while reaping none of the rewards. Work hard and play hard, with his own needs as the goal. That was the motto he'd learned, and he wasn't about to let anything—*anyone*—distract him from it.

He realized Alyssa Hunt was still staring at him and he broke the train of disturbing thoughts. "Let's start with your résumé."

With a firm set to her delectable mouth, she reached into her tote on the floor, pulling out a folder. She handed it to him and silently sat back.

He allowed himself a brief scan of shapely calves and then, with a harsh internal reminder of what this interview was *supposed* to be about, he scanned her résumé instead. And the more he read, the more discouraged he got. When he reached the end, brows pinched with doubt, he met her gaze again.

"Your experience consists of minor corporate functions. Our social events will be on a much larger scale. And certainly more..." He paused, searching for a tactful approach. Wouldn't want to expose her vulnerabilities again, and his unwanted twinge of sympathy. "Sophisticated."

He failed at his task, because her posture and the polite expression went brittle enough to break. But the sexy drawl returned, stronger than before. "I'm perfectly capable of handlin' the work, Mr. Domingues."

He crossed his arms, amused. "I'm sorry to disappoint you." And he meant it. Because the woman fascinated him. But he couldn't let the most important business acquisition of his life hinge on an unqualified event planner, not without supervision. And he'd decided the woman would definitely be a distraction. The thought strengthened his resolve, and he set her résumé on the desk behind him. "Besides, I told you," he went on, "I'm looking for an in-house planner."

Her delicate chin climbed higher, and this time her words were as crisp as her posture. "And I believe as your strategic *partner*, I would make a better choice."

Paulo's lips twitched at her carefully worded description. "I don't do partners." Neither professionally, nor personally. He'd learned both in one neat and tidy bout with betrayal.

So thoughtfully provided to him via his family and his ex-wife.

The memory kicked up a dust cloud of bitterness, choking off his good humor. Seeking a zen-like calm, he picked up the autographed baseball displayed on his desk and rolled it between his hands. Because calm was okay. Actually, calm was good. But forgetting…?

Absolutely not.

So now he limited his relationships to those that went as deep as easy listening Muzak. He liked his women soothing, occasionally diverting, but relegated to the background of his life.

After a few seconds, Paulo realized Alyssa wasn't gathering her tote to leave. If anything, she looked even more rooted in her chair. Interesting.

But, as enjoyable as this interview was, he was late for his meeting with the contractor. With a touch of regret, he pushed up from the desk and set the ball aside. "You have my answer, Ms. Hunt," Paulo said. "My secretary will see you out."

As he headed for the door, he heard her heels hit the wood floor and follow. A surprised grin shot to his lips. Determination appeared to be the lady's first, last and middle name.

"If you would just give me a chance." Alyssa Hunt laid a gentle hand on his arm.

The soft Southern accent and skin-on-skin touch stopped him mid-step, cranking up the achy need with a visceral response that left him smoking. His grin died as he turned to stare at her. Damn. Torture was definitely the order of the day. And while she was busy twisting him in painful knots, her face remained cool and collected.

And how moronic would it be to pass on a planner that could solve his problem? It wouldn't be the first time he'd had to resist the allure of a beautiful woman. She was clearly tenacious, and he could use someone with that much fire on his side.

At the very least he could give her a chance to change his mind. Because his secretary was too overwhelmed to help, and he needed somebody now. Someone who at least had a *clue*. Rubbing his jaw, he considered his next move, and realized he had only one choice.

He would just have to continually beat it into his head not to flirt with the woman.

"Okay, Ms. Hunt." Paulo crossed his arms, breaking their contact and the resulting sizzle, his tone all business. "I have to check the contractor's work in the penthouse." He nodded toward the elevator down the hall, his lips smiling in rebellious anticipation. "You have until we reach the top floor to convince me to hire you."

After two blinks and three pounding heartbeats, the words penetrated Alyssa's brain. Gaping open-mouthed would hardly be polite, but her eyelids managed to do a decent imitation. Because there wouldn't be time to give an address and phone number, much less pull off the impossible.

But at least he'd agreed to hear her pitch. She discreetly bit her lip and looked at Paulo, now dressed in jeans and a black T-shirt. She guessed the wealthy son of a powerful family and owner of a successful line of hotels didn't need a suit. She wished she had that option. With a tiny sigh, she wiggled her toes, cramped in her designer heels.

Perhaps if she pried that silver spoon from his smart-alecky mouth, it would wipe the sexy smile from his face?

Well, she wanted this account and she wasn't giving up. She forced herself to focus. "Okay, Mr. Domingues." He set off down the hallway, and she followed along beside him. "I'm familiar with the boutique concept of your hotel line." They entered the lobby, her heels clicking on the wood, and she went on. "And I admire its emphasis on personal service."

As they crossed the floor, she snuck a peek at Paulo. His face looked almost bored.

Her heart slunk lower as they reached their destination. "I have excellent people skills. I'm committed to customer satisfaction." With the push of a button, the elevator doors opened and they entered. When the doors slid shut behind her, she said, "And I work well under pressure."

This seemed to prick his interest. "Do you really?" he said as he stepped closer.

His proximity, and the smolder in his eyes, pushed her closer to the edge, and every cell in her body ceased what it was doing to take notes. She inhaled, only to catch a whiff of masculine soap.

Easy, Alyssa. Remember what's important.

She forced herself to maintain a neutral expression. "Would you like me to cite specific examples?"

A dimple appeared as he leaned closer, pushing a button on the panel beside her. "I'd rather see for myself."

Was that what this torture session was all about? Palms damp, she felt her stomach lurch as the elevator lifted. A pinging sound began as they passed each floor, coming way too quickly for comfort, but she pressed on. "I'm a stickler for detail. I'm organized and efficient." She made the mistake of lifting her gaze. His face was now two feet away.

And suddenly she was drowning. Drowning in those better-than-mocha-cappuccino eyes. More golden-brown than dark. Beautiful. With tiny little specks of green.

He had to know exactly what he was doing to her as he patiently waited for her to go on. Ignoring the pesky rate of her heart, she searched for a safe focal point, but couldn't find one. "And I'm particularly good at creative solutions to last minute problems," she said.

"A thinking-outside-the-box kinda girl?"

"Definitely."

Ping... His brow lifted expectantly. "Go on."

His mischievous expression morphed gorgeous into irresistible. And although he wasn't even close to touching her, he didn't need to.

He slayed her with a look from those bedroom eyes.

She glanced at the elevator panel, her mind scrambling for something brilliant to say.

Ping... One floor left. A thin line of sweat broke out along her upper lip.

Come on, girl. What's wrong with you? Your goal, remember? To produce the high-end events that lured you into the business in the first place, and to heck with the past.

The last ding sounded in the small compartment.

Alyssa swore under her breath and reached out to push the emergency stop button. The elevator halted with a jolt that had them bracing against the mirrored walls for support.

Paulo's expression shot to one of total surprise. "What are you doing?"

After dedicating every waking moment to her business, indulging in a daydream that included her and a potential client was certainly understandable. It just wasn't acceptable. No matter how tempting. She forced her shoulders back. "I told you. I'm good at creative solutions."

His forehead bunched in suppressed amusement.

But this was her *dream* she was fighting for. Nothing funny about it. "Look, Mr. Domingues. I know every vendor in town for putting on a reception." His amused expression didn't budge. And, really, he was standing entirely too close. "You want exotic flowers? Use Lynn's Boutique. They aren't as fast as Beth's Florals, but worth the wait if you have the time." She sucked in a breath, dizzy from her efforts and the handsome man in front of her. "Catering a seafood buffet? Use Dominic's. Their stuffed scallops are fantastic but they don't do prime rib so well."

A lock of hair fell forward across her face.

Alyssa reached up to brush the strand back into place, Paulo's eyes following her every move. And by the end of the maneuver his gaze was dark. Even as she fought the rising tide of awareness, she knew it was hopeless. The surge of desire had swelled to new heights. Enveloping her. Fogging her brain.

"But whatever you do…" The tight sound of her voice was foreign, but the familiar twang was thick. "Don't order your ice carvin' from Jenny's Designs." Alyssa waited for him to ask why, but Paulo just stared at her. Was he even listening anymore? Nerves stretched to the max, she pressed on, answering the unasked question. "Their sculptures suck."

Paulo let out a low chuckle. "That wasn't a very professional critique."

"I tried professional." She frowned. "But you weren't paying attention."

"Oh, trust me." He took half a step closer, sending heat slithering along her veins. "I'm definitely paying attention."

Hypnotized, she tried to become one with the elevator, pressing her back against the door. Wicked messages skittered like skipping stones along her every nerve. Because that mouth would entice the strongest of women.

And, sadly, she was learning she wasn't as strong as she thought. She longed to run a finger along his lower lip and then drop her hand to the awe-inspiring plane of muscle on his chest. The mirrored elevator would certainly provide an atmosphere for incredible sex. A person could see everything. And making love with this man would rate a category five on the hurricane rating scale.

"Time's up," he said.

His gaze radiated a heat hotter than the sands of South Miami Beach at high noon, and Alyssa watched in utter amazement as Paulo slowly leaned forward.

Did he think he could just *kiss* her?

Those hazel eyes, those wonderful, heavy, sexy eyes, lingered on her mouth. Molten lava pooled, shortcircuiting her brain. His lips were full, sensual, and slightly parted.

Closer…

His left arm lifted. Where was that hand going?

Closer…

"You'd better brace yourself," he said huskily.

Her body's reaction to his words prevented any hope of a coherent thought, and his meaning didn't become clear until she heard the pop of the emergency button beside her. But by then it was too late, and when the doors slid open she began to fall.

CHAPTER TWO

PAULO stepped forward to catch Alyssa just as her fingers clutched his shirt, and, like a Jackie Chan swivel kick to the chest, the contact blasted his intentions to smithereens.

His body cataloged every glorious sensation. The intoxicating feel of her gentle hips beneath his hands. The knuckles flat against him. But her thighs pressed to his were the most disrupting. Everything about him was hard, while she was soft, supple, bringing sultry visions of hot Southern nights. Entwined limbs. And sated bodies.

He'd wanted to know if the attraction was mutual, but the expression that flashed on her face when her gaze dropped to his mouth…

Man, some things a guy just couldn't be held responsible for.

So he'd opened the door to escape her and get his reaction under control, triggering a nuclear explosion.

He seized hold of his response and cleared his throat. "Next time someone tells you to brace yourself, you should listen," Paulo said as he slowly set her back, ignoring the protests from his body. She released his shirt, but her frozen expression gave him no inkling what she'd do next. At this point, all he knew was to expect the unexpected from this woman. He lifted a brow. "Are you planning on following me into the penthouse?"

Something flickered across her face he couldn't interpret.

Maybe awareness tinged with annoyance? "There's nothing I need to see in the penthouse," she said with a slight frown.

His lips twitched at the tone that implied he'd meant something lurid. Or maybe that was his libido providing the translation. Hell, he shouldn't tease her either, but he couldn't help himself. "Oh, I definitely have something you want to see." He suppressed the grin and headed for the door at the end of the hall.

Watching her deliver her presentation, the cool demeanor slowly slipping away and the occasional—and increasingly stronger—hint of attraction, had been the highlight of his month. Maybe the last three months. At least until the pull became so magnetic the need to push her up against the wall and kiss the reserved professional right out of her had all but overwhelmed him.

As he neared the suite, he heard her scurry down the hall behind him just before she joined him at the door.

With a lift of her chin, the poise was back. "We've reached the top, Mr. Domingues. My pitch is over. Do I have the job or not?"

Paulo propped a shoulder against the wall, struck with the need to keep her as off balance as he felt. And if she tipped that chin at him one more time, pretending she didn't return the attraction, he'd forget his good intentions and take the kiss he'd been dying for during their riveting ride up. "Too busy to take in the view from the penthouse, huh?"

A myriad of emotions crossed her face, as if she was baffled how to handle their interaction.

Welcome to the club, lady.

Finally, she sent him an overly patient look. "Not everyone is born with money to burn."

He bit back the grin at her indirect slur. "And I'm not convinced you have the necessary skills to handle this job."

"I can do this job better than anyone else you can find."

His eyebrows shot higher. She had zero experience in social events. And her confidence amused him. "Can you?"

"Definitely."

He continued to hold back the smile. He was enjoying the exchange way too much. And he'd made the decision to hire her the second she'd hit the stop button in the elevator.

But after the desertion of his old event planner and the band for the grand opening, he felt the need to make a point. It was imperative she follow through. He had no tolerance for false promises, employees who talked big but failed to deliver.

He tipped his head and went on. "I have a little task that needs attention. In six months the mayor is having her fiftieth birthday party at the Samba. Nothing has been done on it yet." He maintained a straight face, despite the lie. "Do you think you could prepare a complete event proposal?"

"Naturally."

The corner of his mouth twitched in amusement. "Can you have it ready by tomorrow?"

Her eyelids flared briefly, and she hesitated. He could almost see the smoke from the wheels turning in her brain. No doubt trying to come up with a tactful way to tell him to go to hell. He waited, itching to hear her carefully worded no.

"Of course," she finally said.

His amusement came to an abrupt end. It was an impossible task, and she should know that. As he stared at Alyssa, for a moment he considered changing his mind about hiring her, wondering if she suffered from delusions of grandeur. But he'd laid out his plan, and until she signed a contract he wasn't stuck with a crazy employee.

And he absolutely *had* to see what she would come up with next.

"Good," he said with a sharp nod. "Until I'm confident in your skills, you'll be under the supervision of my manager. But, assuming your references hold up, you're hired." He finally pushed away from the wall. "On your way out, stop by and see my secretary to sign the permission form for a reference and background check."

Alyssa Hunt went so still she could have doubled as a photograph.

What now? Had she had a fight with a former client? He bit back the grin, imagining the incident. "Shall I escort you back to the reception desk?"

With a small frown, Alyssa hiked her tote higher and looked at him coolly. "I'm perfectly capable of finding my way."

His grin finally reappeared. "I have no doubt you are."

Clever little bastard. Who the heck did he think she was? A naive country bumpkin who didn't know the score? As if the accent she couldn't completely suppress somehow made her gullible. She hated being stereotyped.

Happy to finally have exchanged the restricting suit for her well-worn jeans, Alyssa leaned back on the leather couch in her apartment. She propped her bare feet on the glass coffee table, wiggling her still hurting toes, glad to be free of the designer high heels.

Why couldn't they design a little comfort into their hideously expensive shoes? If people weren't so fixated on external image, she wouldn't bother with the dreaded torture traps. Of course, the casual style Paulo sported suited him. He looked like a bazillion bucks with no effort at all.

She blew out a breath and sank deeper into the couch.

And his "little" task, as he so casually labeled it, couldn't be done in one night. And certainly not without interviewing the mayor. She'd smelled the trap the moment he asked for the proposal by tomorrow. But why? To get her to admit it was impossible? To see how much she knew?

Peeved, she'd blurted out her response, preparing to go home and do the best she could by gleaning a little info about the mayor off the internet. It wouldn't be her finest work, just a rough idea to get things started.

And then she'd discovered it was completely unnecessary.

Irritation surged again as she remembered her conversation with his secretary. Figuring her meeting with the woman should be put to good use, Alyssa had asked her about the upcoming party. And learned that, sitting in a file in Paulo's office, was the previous event planner's completed proposal.

And a pretty good one, too. Alyssa knew that for a fact. Because she'd seen it.

Fuming at what Paulo probably thought was cute little ploy to test her, she'd sent the secretary up to the penthouse to ask him a question and then snuck into his office, found the file, and made a copy.

Alyssa looked at the document splayed across her coffee table. Now that she had all the notes about the mayor's preferences, and the event planner's ideas, Alyssa couldn't decide what to do with the information.

Chewing on the tip of a nail, she eyed the papers, pondering her next move.

It was a decent proposal. With a few tweaks of the less inspiring elements, and some computer-generated graphics, it had the makings of a humdinger of a report. And if she didn't change it too much, Paulo would recognize his former employee's work.

A small smile slipped up her face as she pictured him stumped, trying to figure out how she'd gotten hold of the file. He wouldn't, of course. Avoiding the discreet security camera in the lobby had been the perfect test of her expertise.

Not that she was particularly proud of her childhood skills. But, with the background check, Paulo was going to find out about her criminal record anyway.

With a sigh of resignation, she dropped her head back to rest on the couch.

When she'd started her business, with the first three jobs

she'd gone after she'd been completely honest, telling the prospective clients about her history. It was in the past. She wasn't that person anymore. And she refused to hide in shame.

But the information had lost her every one of those accounts.

After that, she hadn't volunteered a thing. And not one of her clients had asked for a formal background check since. Until today.

A familiar feeling of defeat threatened to swamp her, but she pushed it aside. One thing she knew for sure: the secret to dealing with Paulo Domingues was to never let him get the upper hand. Always leave him guessing. Keep the cocky man just a little unsure of himself. So she'd show him exactly who Alyssa Hunt was.

Someone who wasn't afraid to take him on, tit for tat. *Mano a womano.*

And if he was going to change his mind about hiring her because of her history anyway, well...then she'd go out in a blaze of glory.

With a renewed determination, Alyssa sat up and reached for the copy of the proposal.

At seven forty-five the next morning, Alyssa sat in a cab on the way to the Samba, cradling her latte with its potent double shot of caffeine. Sleep had been in short supply last night, but there had been plenty of room for work.

And now that she knew she found Paulo attractive, that he bound her insides up so tight blood could barely find its way to her toes, she'd skipped the designer shoes for less torturous heels. There was only so much constriction a girl could take. Unfortunately, her taupe pantsuit wasn't comfortable either. But today, to provide her ensemble with a little flair, she'd added a Prada tote. At least it didn't inflict pain.

A squeak of tires sounded as the taxi slowed and stopped at the curb. Alyssa grabbed her things and climbed out onto the sidewalk, giving the door a solid push. The decisive smack was a jolting boost to her courage. She had her proposal, her laptop, and enough caffeine on board to keep her charged for weeks.

After marching up the steps, she pulled open the heavy door and entered the spacious lobby. Stainless steel and stone accents lent a modern touch. Gleaming hardwood floors added warmth. And in the center of it all a huge bar was set against a slate backdrop, water sheeting down the rock wall. The soothing murmur provided a cool place to escape the scorching tropical sun with frosty drink in hand.

And she could use a little soothing because, when she spied Paulo approaching, her body reacted with a mixture of heat, dread, and mutinous anticipation.

Alyssa brushed her hair from her cheek, composing herself.

"Good morning." He stopped in front of her and studied her closely. He wore black jeans and a white dress shirt, sleeves rolled to the elbows, his well-muscled forearms displayed in all their glory. "You're much too young to have dark shadows under your eyes, Ms. Hunt."

"At twenty-eight, I'm much too old to be called young," she said. "And anyway, youth does not preclude a person from hard work." Lord knows she was living proof.

"Work? That's the cause of the circles?" He shook his head, and a wave of gorgeous, devil-may-care hair fell across his forehead. "I thought maybe you'd thrown your proposal together and then stayed up late having fun with friends." With a smile, he went on. "Or maybe with a date."

She forced her brow to relax. He really did think he was cute. And after their elevator ride, rife with sexual tension, clarifying her position on *that* particular topic would be smart. Like the fact she refused to be tempted by his charms. "I'm too focused on my company to date."

His eyes narrowed. "You don't date," he repeated slowly, as

if unable to digest her statement. "So you either sustain yourself on a string of one-night stands or you're celibate."

Damn. How had the conversation taken such a radical turn? Alyssa raised a single brow as delicately as she could. "You have a rather limited take on the concept of dating."

He looked amused. "It doesn't begin and end with sex, true. But it should at least include it." His eyes crinkled in question. "Are you seriously forgoing a social life for work?"

Gone were the teasing undertones, and the genuine curiosity in his expression made her feel like an oddball. Her nonexistent sex life hadn't been a conscious decision, only one of necessity. Once she began her business, she hadn't had time for the kind of relationship that went deep enough for that kind of intimacy.

Not to mention there was always the sticky issue of her past.

But unfortunately it appeared declaring her lifestyle up-front had only piqued his interest instead of squashing it. Really, the man should come with an instruction manual.

Buck up, Alyssa. You can be cool. You can be elegant.

After securing her hair behind her ear, she smiled politely and turned the topic back to safer waters. "Don't we have business to discuss?"

"Straight to the job at hand." The killer grin returned with a flash. "I like that."

He placed a hand under her elbow, the assault on her senses cutting off her response. Smooth skin caressed her arm as he steered Alyssa toward the staff area. She tried to ignore his touch, the heat, and the memories of yesterday. It didn't go so well.

Paulo guided her down a hall with offices on either side—the largest of which was his—to a doorway at the end. He stopped and held out an arm. "This space was reserved for the event planner's use."

She entered the room, and her jaw went slack in surprise. The office wasn't huge, but the exquisitely crafted cherry desk, dark wood filing cabinets and Persian rug that lay between were lovely. No, *beautiful.* And it sure beat the dining room in her apartment. She set her bag down and touched the desk longingly, aware of Paulo's eyes on her.

"But as an in-house planner," Paulo added, "she worked exclusively for the Samba."

The words spurred her to face him, and Alyssa frowned. Was he suggesting she would take advantage of the space? "You don't need to worry I'll abuse my privileges, Mr. Domingues. I'm a professional."

His gaze didn't waver. "Being a professional doesn't make up for your lack of experience." As the seconds ticked by, they stared at each other—a silent battle of wills—before Paulo went on. "So why don't you show me your ideas for the mayor's birthday party."

A ghost of a smile formed as Alyssa reached into her bag and withdrew the work she had spent yesterday afternoon and a good part of the night putting together. The new and improved proposal, reprinted on *her* business letterhead.

"Of course." Alyssa held out the document, complete with the added glossy photos and sketches.

Paulo's expression was worth every minute of lost sleep.

She boldly held his gaze and continued. "My ideas, as requested."

With a stunned look, he accepted the folder, and she went on in a brisk, businesslike tone. "I also have a detailed cost analysis. In case the client chooses to go with the proposal." It took all she had not to giggle as she passed him the second document.

Paulo took the report, disbelief radiating from his face. "How did you manage all this?"

"I told you." Game. Set. And end of the match. *Ha!* "I can do this job better than anyone else you can find."

Long moments ticked by as he flipped through the documents, his movements growing slower and slower. She knew the second he recognized the information, because an unmistakable look of understanding flashed in his eyes. After another pause, he carefully set the reports on the desk before turning back to her. "Impressive," he said.

That would teach him not to underestimate her, hick accent or not.

She sent him her best "aww, shucks" smile and fluttered her eyelashes, just a touch, for effect. "Thank you."

In response, a glint of amusement flared in his eyes. "You did all this without help?"

She could fess up. Give it to him straight. But something held her back. Maybe it was the way he kept challenging her. Let him figure it out all by his little ol' self.

"I told you," she said, eyeing him levelly, "I'm good at creative solutions."

Take that, Mr. Smooth-Talking Charmer.

His lips twisted, and he tipped his head up. For a moment, he looked as if he would burst out laughing. Instead, he wiped a hand down his mouth and stepped closer—*too* close—and Alyssa's awareness shot from coffee shop grande to extra-venti.

There was no denying he was good at the counterpoint move.

Frozen in place, she gripped the desk behind her and resisted the urge to shrink away, holding her breath. Unfortunately she didn't think to stop breathing until after she'd caught a whiff of his scent...sandalwood, mixed with desire, and a generous dose of danger.

"*Very* creative, I see," he said. "Are you sure you produced the reports single-handedly?" His right eyebrow climbed a tiny degree higher, as if waiting for her to respond. "No help from any..." He paused, as if allowing her time to fill in the blank. Heart thumping madly, she forced herself to maintain his gaze, a cool smile plastered on her face. "Friends?" he finished.

Due to his scent and his nearness, it took several seconds for her muddled brain to send a message to the muscles in charge of her mouth. "None whatsoever."

Paulo slowly leaned forward, reaching for something on the desk behind her, his six-foot-plus frame dwarfing hers. Her nerves scrambled for cover as he came close enough to almost touch her. Thick eyelashes and sensual lips brought memories of yesterday's elevator ride. And then he straightened up, holding out a file. "Our contract."

When she managed to take it, he folded his arms across his chest and turned to sit on the desk, creating enough space for her to breathe again. And the look that crossed his face told her she was in trouble.

He cleared his throat. "In light of your…" pausing, he pursed his lips for a moment before going on "…*superior* performance, I've decided your work won't be supervised by my manager."

"Excuse me?" Shoot—the drawl again.

There was no smile, only an expression bordering on a smirk. "You'll be reporting to me."

A bolt of electrical energy deep-fried her nerve-endings. Alyssa chewed on her lip and willed her heart back to a reasonable rate. Her little deed had earned her the eagle eye of the boss instead of an immediate firing. But didn't he have better things to do than torment his new event planner?

Paulo cocked his head. She couldn't tell what he was thinking, but at least his tone was businesslike. "Do we have a deal?"

Alyssa rounded the desk, not stopping until it was between her and Paulo. It was much easier to handle him from a distance. And her voice was clearer, too. "Of course."

"Good," he said, and then headed for the door. "I have a few things to discuss with my secretary." He stopped at the threshold and turned to face her. His eyes communicated exactly what he wanted to see the woman about. The file. The twinkle appeared in his eyes again. "Anything you want to tell me before I go?"

"No," she said coolly. "Not a thing."

The light in his eyes grew brighter as he acknowledged the stalemate with a sharp nod. "Okay. I'll be back to see how you're doing at the end of the day." And then he turned and headed out the exit.

Alyssa flopped into her chair and dropped her head back, staring at the door he'd closed behind him. Oh, joy. He was coming back to check on her. More nerve-racking moments to look forward to. This game of cat and mouse was doable until he stepped closer and she could *feel* the attraction, an almost physical presence. It was like being caught in a tractor beam.

Sucking her in.

And on the off chance her background check didn't get her fired, now her job would involve daily direct contact with Paulo Domingues. *Daily direct contact.*

How in the world was she going to handle the constant scrutiny of the bedeviling man? Even more crucial, how was she going to survive the undeniable way he made her feel?

"Look," Nick Tatum said. His sandy brown hair stuck out beneath the baseball cap perched backward on his head. "Right there." Paulo's friend hit the pause button on the security video, and an image of Alyssa from yesterday froze on the TV. She was standing at the reception desk of the Samba, in her boring gray suit. "Do you see that?" Nick pointed at Alyssa's right hand where it rested on the counter. "Her fingers are angled in a different position."

Paulo frowned and leaned in for a closer look at the screen.

Right after he'd spoken with his secretary, he called Nick. Friends since junior high, there was no one Paulo trusted more. For the last twenty minutes they'd been reviewing the tape in the security guard's tiny office, and Paulo's frustration was mounting. "That doesn't prove anything."

After calling a few of her former clients yesterday, every one of them singing her praises, Paulo had decided Alyssa might be able to cut the mustard. When she'd handed over the mountain of work she achieved overnight, his fascination had reached for the roof.

And the thought of leaving her supervision to Charles had left him feeling cheated.

At first he'd assumed she'd asked the secretary for the report, but that had turned up false. Then he'd thought she'd helped herself to the file from his office. But when he'd found the document in his filing cabinet, he'd run into a dead end. The security tape was supposed to give him the answer. And still he had nothing.

"It doesn't make any sense," Paulo said.

"I'm telling you." In cutoffs and a T-shirt, Nick leaned back, pulling his bowl of popcorn from the table and balancing it on his lap. "She took the file."

"But the file is still in the cabinet."

"Dude." Nick popped a piece of popcorn in his mouth. "She copied it."

"There wasn't time." Aggravated he couldn't solve the perplexing mystery, Paulo raked a hand through his hair. "She had to pull the document from my filing cabinet, use the copier in the staff hallway, return the papers to the office, and then get back to the counter. But every passing sweep of the security camera clearly shows she never left the reception desk."

Crunching on his snack, Nick frowned, as if disappointed by the huge hole in his theory.

"Unless…" Paulo said, a slow realization dawning as he glanced at the watch on her wrist. Why hadn't he thought of it before? "She knew exactly when the camera would be making its sweep, timing her movements to return to stand at the counter at precisely the same spot between each task." He lifted a brow in triumph and glanced at his friend.

Nick's eyes went wide as he let out a low whistle. "Now, *that's* cool." He gazed at the TV screen. "Who'd she organize parties for in the past? The *Mission: Impossible* team?" After a moment's pause, he sent Paulo a grin, his green eyes lit with humor. "If I'd known your workday was this entertaining, I would have hung out here more often."

Entertaining. His new event planner had pulled off a heist in broad daylight, and, short of dusting for fingerprints, Paulo couldn't prove a thing. Granted, she hadn't actually stolen anything, and it would have been information she would have had access to anyway, but that wasn't the point. The point was…

Paulo's thoughts trailed off as he stared at the beautiful woman on the monitor. He couldn't remember his point anymore.

Nick tossed a kernel into the air, caught it in his mouth, and then wagged his finger in the direction of the video recorder. "Let's rewind the tape and watch it again."

Paulo shot Nick a wry look. "Glad you're enjoying the midday movie."

"You're just ticked she bested you at your game."

No, he wasn't. And that was the problem. He wasn't angry; he was massively, massively intrigued by his new event planner's cunning and finesse.

Intrigued and attracted. Not a reassuring combination.

Paulo was saved from dwelling on the growing concern when his cellular phone beeped, and he pulled it from his pocket. Scanning the text message, he felt his snowballing curiosity reach gargantuan proportions. "The results of her background check," he said, waving his phone in the air. "Ten years ago she was convicted of stealing."

They both turned to view the woman on the screen.

After a moment's pause, Nick said, "Why would she risk a stunt that could trigger a look at her record?"

It was the first question Paulo had a ready response to. Eyes fixated on his new event planner, Paulo answered, "She's sending me a message. She doesn't care if I know."

The ticking of the clock on the wall was loud, until Nick finally broke the shocked silence. “Wow. I think I’m in love.” His tone proved just how impressed he was. “If you fire her, I’m hiring her at my club.”

And miss out on the most exciting woman he’d ever met? Not a chance in hell. Paulo continued to stare at Alyssa’s image. “She doesn’t want to be one of your many girlfriends.” He shot Nick a quick look from the corner of his eye. “And I financed that club, remember?”

“And to return the favor I found you the perfect replacement band for the opening of the Samba.” Nick stood and set his popcorn aside. “Seven o’clock. Old Beachside Park. Be there tonight and you can hear their stuff.”

Right now Paulo was too distracted to think of much outside his new employee. He stood, arms crossed, absorbed by her demeanor on the screen. Her posture was dignified as she waited at the counter, her tote hanging from her shoulder. Very professional. How had she retained such a calm expression during her caper?

“Ahem.” Nick waved his hand in front of Paulo’s eyes. “Beachside Park? Seven o’clock?” Paulo turned to face Nick. His friend looked amused as he continued. “Maybe I should just leave the two of you alone.”

Paulo ignored the comment. “I’ll go see the band tonight,” he said. He was more wound up than he’d realized. “Thanks for finding them. I owe you big time.”

Nick shot him a grin. “Always good to keep my obnoxiously rich friend indebted to me. Could come in handy again someday.”

Paulo let out a soft snort. “You’re such a moron.”

“Coming from you, that means nothing,” Nick said, and then his grin grew bigger. “Now I’ll let you get back to your new girlfriend.” After a salute, he headed out the door, chuckling all the way down the hall as he left.

Paulo returned his gaze to the monitor, taking in the curve of Alyssa's backside, the slim calves and the delicate ankles above the spectacular shoes.

Who was this unflappable lady that had descended like Wonder Woman upon his hotel, promising to solve his problem? A woman with enough poise to greet the Queen of England, enough spunk to take on Hell's Angels, and the ability to fight dirty when pushed into a corner.

But she hadn't hidden what she'd done. Instead she'd flaunted it. Gleefully waved it under his nose. Daring him to say something.

While most aggressive go-getters learned to think outside the box, she upped the ante and thought outside of the whole shipping container. And he was developing a deep admiration for his wily new employee.

Admiration, intrigue *and* attraction.

Man, he really was in trouble.

At six-thirty that evening Paulo sat on his motorcycle in front of the Samba, waiting for Alyssa to show. Traffic zipped by on Ocean Drive. Pedestrians meandered along the terracotta walkway, passing hotels and trendy shops, enjoying the cooler evening breeze.

Alyssa appeared and headed down the front steps of the hotel, turning north on the sidewalk. Her respectable pantsuit was paired with a purse that added a bit of chic. Yesterday it was the shoes; today it was her bag. And, though she handled herself with decorum, he was beginning to get a better taste of the woman beneath.

A delicious concoction he'd never encountered before.

As he watched her walk, his eyes dropped to her feet. Before she'd left the building, she had exchanged her heels for a pair of athletic shoes. Interesting.

He started his bike and pulled up beside her, flipping up the visor on his helmet. "I like the new shoes," Paulo said as he balanced the slow-moving motorcycle with his feet. "If you're going home on foot, I can give you a lift."

She kept walking and sent him a tight thanks-but-no-thanks smile. "I'm fine."

"You must be tired after producing such a detailed report."

She ignored his dig and continued her sexy saunter on the sidewalk.

He tried again. "Do you always work this late?"

"The more I get done now, the more time to solicit new events later." She turned to look at him as she continued on her way.

His eyes dropped to take in the translucent pink of her lipstick. The fierce need those full lips created was enough to require a "caution—contents hot" label.

"More events, more income," she said. "I'm sure you understand the benefits of more income."

The words triggered a cascade of memories, every one of them leaving an acrid taste in his mouth. Profit had been the singular concern at Domingues International. But no matter how much he'd added to the bottom line, busting a gut, sacrificing everything to match his brother at work, he'd never obtained that elusive Holy Grail: his father's recognition.

He pushed the bitter thoughts aside, turning his focus back to the feminine challenge before him. "Your long hours are none of my business. All the better for me, I suppose. But personally, I don't think work is worth ruining your health over."

Alyssa stopped mid-step. "Poverty doesn't increase your lifespan either," she said dryly.

Paulo halted beside her, taking a quick glance at her bag, amused. "Is Prada the latest trend among the destitute?"

Her lips quirked, as if holding back a smile. "I bought it secondhand."

"Chic, yet frugal." He stared at her, more intrigued than ever. But what did he expect? A confession that she'd swiped it?

"That's a rare female combination of traits." Everything about this woman was exceptional.

"As the daughter of a teenage mother working for minimum wage, I didn't have much of a choice," Alyssa said, and started up the sidewalk again.

Hmm, now he was getting somewhere. Because he was burning with curiosity about her past. With his twist of the throttle, the motorcycle revved in response, and he pulled forward on the road to follow along beside her again. "I imagine that was a tough way to grow up."

A small smile graced her lips, but she didn't turn to look at him. "No offense, Mr. Domingues," she said as she continued her stroll, her silky hair swinging against her shoulders. "But I really don't think *you* can."

Paulo grinned. He got a kick out of her refreshingly sassy mouth that kept lobbing subtle barbs in his direction. There was no resentment in her tone. Nor any sign of anger. Only a slight impatience, as if she was in possession of super-secret knowledge he wasn't privy to.

With the roaring pop of a wheelie, he pulled up on the sidewalk in front of her, and had the pleasure of seeing a startled look fly to her face as she came to a halt. "I have to check out a potential band for the grand opening," he said. Pleased by her expression, he struggled to keep a straight face. "As my new event planner, you should be there." While she stared at him, he sent her a measured look as he tipped his head toward the back of his bike. "Hop on."

CHAPTER THREE

ALYSSA looked down at the candy-apple-red, ultra-modern motorcycle, more suited for a racetrack than a city street, and her body reacted. Heart stomping. Stomach swirling. Nerves churning. She hoped her eyes didn't resemble those of a tree frog. "You want me to ride there on *that*?"

His look was deceptively bland beneath the matching red helmet. "It's just a Ducati. It doesn't bite."

As she continued to eye it dubiously, he straightened up, balancing the idling motorcycle between his legs. "Are you afraid?"

The hint of an I-dare-you tone and the suggestive question pricked a nerve. "Of you—no," she said firmly, hoping to convince herself. She wrestled with the alarming and distressingly heady idea of touching him again. "Of splattering my brains on the pavement—yes." It seemed a logical enough excuse.

With a look of suppressed humor, Paulo took off his helmet and held it out in offering, waiting patiently.

"What about you?" she said.

The angular, masculine features, combined with the waves of hair and Latino coloring, made him hot enough to star on the silver screen. "I'll risk it."

Her lids dropped to half-mast. "I just bet you will."

Unfortunately, he'd addressed her safety concerns. Any more excuses would look too obvious. And he was right; she needed to be there to hear the band. Blowing out a breath, she wordlessly accepted the helmet and clamped it on her head. After securing her bag on her shoulder, she threw her leg over the back of the bike. She leaned forward, struggling to hold on to Paulo with dignity and still keep her distance.

"Hang on tight." Paulo pulled her arms firmly around him, spooning her body against his.

The surefire kick to the solar plexus restricted air entry into her lungs. Every solid inch of him was hard, from the back plastered against her breast, to the chest beneath her arms and the thighs between her legs. Alyssa fought for breath as Paulo twisted the throttle, and with a rumbling whine they were off.

For the next few minutes she concentrated on the view of the Atlantic and the sun on her shoulders while trying to rein in her response. The decadent agony ended when Paulo stopped at a park bustling with people and dismounted.

He nodded toward an ice cream vendor. "Vanilla or chocolate?"

Alyssa paused in the midst of pulling off the helmet, a smile of surprise threatening to hijack her mouth. The handsome man wearing a rakish expression looked more inclined to buy her a beer or a whiskey or a Blue 32 shooter. Ice cream sounded so innocent.

"Vanilla," she said.

While he made their purchases, Alyssa headed toward one of the few empty benches and sat down. When Paulo joined her, he handed her a vanilla cone and kept a chocolate for himself, taking a seat beside her. Desperate to ignore his proximity, she studied the scene.

Sun sparkling off its surface, the Atlantic Ocean spread out before them in shifting shades of blue moving from aquamarine to dark indigo as the ocean floor dropped away. People in shorts and bathing suits milled about on grass dotted with palm trees, while the band set up their equipment on the outdoor stage.

One by one her muscles relaxed, her posture easing against the seat. And the vanilla treat tasted like heaven.

After a few minutes, Paulo interrupted the silence. “Where did you grow up?”

Alyssa tensed. *Here we go. Time for the third degree.* She turned to look at him as calmly as she could. “I thought you didn’t need to pump me for information?”

A dimple popped into view. “Maybe I spoke too soon.”

The nonchalant words were harmless enough, but she wasn’t fooled. And she wouldn’t volunteer anything more than he asked directly. “I was born in Okeechobee County and moved to Miami when I was five.”

“A country girl at heart, huh?”

“Country. City.” She shrugged and sent him a pointed look. “I prefer not to be characterized in such a shallow way.”

A second dimple popped into view. “How would you characterize yourself?”

She met his gaze, refusing to give anything away. “As an excellent businesswoman.”

“Any other traits I should be aware of?”

Alyssa’s brow pulled tight as her words from their first meeting were being thrown back in her face. And as she studied him—the expression, the knowledge in his eyes—she knew. He’d run the check and heard about her record. Asking her to come see the band was an excuse.

She was about to get canned. Again.

With the bellowing dive alarm of a submarine, her stomach descended to her toes. Her dream job was coming to an end before it began. And she was so tired of being labeled by her past. So very, very tired.

But she wasn’t going to cower like a coward. She crossed her legs, summoning every ounce of poise she possessed. “For a self-described straight shooter, you beat around the bush a lot,

Mr. Domingues," she said. "Why don't you just tell me what's on your mind."

"I read about your conviction."

Though her heart pounded, her gaze didn't flinch. She hated excuses, and she wasn't about to offer him one. But she hated being defined by that moment even more. And what was she supposed to say? She hiked an eyebrow. "So...?"

Paulo loosely shrugged a shoulder, as if it were no big deal. "So, I want to learn more."

His casual attitude toward the issue grated, and irritation flared, reflected in her tone. "The rest is none of your damn business."

He leaned back in surprise, whether from her cuss word or her response, she wasn't sure. "You're my employee," he said.

As if that entitled him to dig into her most private moments.

"I'm your *partner*," she said.

"I told you," he said easily. "I don't do partners. Especially ones I can't trust."

Irritation made way for anger, skewering her insides further. Ten years later and the whole world refused to let her move on. Tethered her to the past like she was a mangy dog. No matter how hard she worked, it meant nothing. Emotion had the words tumble unchecked from her lips, her accent strong.

"I made some mistakes. I paid for my crimes." She sat up higher in her seat. "But I can produce the kind of events that will knock the socks off your guests. If you're going to fire me, Mr. Domingues, then do it. Otherwise—" she sent him a frown "—quit jerkin' me around."

He lifted his lips into another crooked smile. "I don't want to fire you."

The words knocked her off kilter, defusing her anger with a single sentence. Her brow shot upward of its own accord. "You don't?"

"Do you still steal?"

Confused, she frowned harder. "No."

His smile grew bigger. "Then we don't have a problem."

He wasn't going to fire her like the others.

Dumbfounded by the unexpected turn of events, she slowly settled back against the bench and turned her face toward the crowd, feeling overwhelmed. No matter how much she hadn't wanted to care, a part of her had always been hurt by the clients who changed their minds about her when they learned the truth. Sad they couldn't see beyond her mistakes to the hard-working woman she was now. She had poured everything she had into her business.

Impatient with herself, she blinked back the sting of tears, refusing to let him see her cry. She didn't want his pity. Concentrating on the scene, she watched the band began to warm up, listening to the chords as the lead singer strummed his guitar.

Paulo was her first client not to boot her to the door after the news. Of the three others, two had given her a false smile and excuses about why she wasn't right for the job, while the third had been more up-front. She preferred the honest approach. After two years of suffering at the hands of her snooty, rich college classmates, she had no patience left for false airs and pretense. But, rich as he was, Paulo Domingues didn't fall into that category.

Honestly, she had no idea what category he belonged to anymore.

She finally composed herself and found her voice. "If you aren't going to fire me, why are you pushing me so hard for information?"

He leaned forward, his face lit with curiosity. "I want to know how you got hold of that file."

So it wasn't her record that bothered him. It was not knowing how she'd pulled off her cheat. Despite the lingering emotion, delight spread through her body. At this point she'd work for him for free, just for the fun of keeping him on his toes. She widened her eyes innocently. "What file?"

His lips quirked as he stared at her a moment more. "Never mind. The details aren't important. I've learned enough for today." He shifted on the bench, his knee pressing against hers, and a nervous thrill skittered along her limbs. "Like the way your drawl gets heavy and that cool exterior slips when you're angry." His gaze traveled across her face, and the transformation to lazy charm was instantaneous. "It also happens when you're fighting the attraction between us."

Her heart tripped before picking up speed.

With a hard swallow, she refused to look away. Because that would be admitting he was right. And as she met his gaze, she could feel the old awareness rise from the ashes like a phoenix. She clutched her cone, back rigid, as a breeze blew her hair across her face, partially veiling her vision. But Alyssa couldn't move. And, no matter how much he knew, acknowledging it out loud had to be a bad idea.

"I think you're confusing irritation with attraction," she said, shooting for a lofty, confident air, but knowing she fell horribly short.

His eyes went dark. "Am I?" he said as he swept the hair from her face, his fingers lingering on her cheek.

A shower of shivers coursed down her spine, and the resulting blaze melted the tension in her back and muddled her brain. She was vaguely aware ice cream dripped onto her fingers. But the cold droplets did little to extinguish the heat in her body. She sat, paralyzed, as his eyes dropped to her lips, increasing her internal Fahrenheit reading to the boiling point.

"A challenge like that is impossible to resist," he murmured.

Alyssa's breath paused in her throat while he slowly lowered his head, as if he was reconsidering his actions along the way. But when his mouth touched hers, he came alive and opened her lips wide. Boldly invading the soft recesses. Taking what he wanted. And the demand for submission kicked her reaction into overdrive.

She leaned into the kiss. The taste of sweet vanilla mixed with rich chocolate as his tongue mated with hers, an act that left her achy with need. Fire swirled like a tornado in her stomach, creating a force that pulled the warmth down, concentrating the heat between her legs. Lordy, her *body* was melting…

Wanting more, needing more, with a groan she gripped his shirt, her response taking on a quality too sinful for a public place.

And then Paulo pulled back, his breathing heavy, his eyes darkly curious. “Exactly how long has your ban on dating been going on?”

Every nerve working overtime, she released his shirt and tucked her hair behind her ear, fingers trembling from the shock and awe to her senses. She swiped a napkin down the hand holding the cone, pretending to be concerned about the drips of ice cream before recovering enough to meet his gaze. “That’s none of your business either.”

“I disagree,” he said. “It’s very much my business.” He lifted a meaningful brow. “Because your sweet-as-molasses drawl is thick when you’re turned on.”

It was just a silly little kiss.

Fingers wrapped around the handle, Alyssa stared into her open refrigerator, the cool air seeping in her direction. But her body was still hot. She wasn’t hungry for breakfast, and gazing blankly at the shelves, continuing to pretend she wasn’t affected by yesterday’s events, wasn’t helping. With a frown, she finally closed the door.

Time to admit the kiss hadn’t been little and was far, far from silly. But it was only a temporary lapse. A one-time slip-up. Obviously abstinence was affecting her reactions.

Fortunately, after listening to the first couple of songs, Paulo had decided the band was perfect, and Alyssa had been more than eager to leave. Sitting next to him, trying to concentrate on the music, had left her antsy. When he had offered her a ride home, she'd politely declined and taken a taxi.

Unfortunately, the scorching encounter had left her coiled tighter than the box springs beneath her mattress. Sleep had been impossible.

If she wasn't careful, her business would start to suffer.

Her cell phone buzzed on the dining room table, and she crossed the kitchen to pick it up. "Elite Events."

"Lyssa."

At the familiar sound of her mother's syrupy voice, Alyssa knew the conversation wouldn't be quick. She clamped her phone between her ear and her shoulder, gathering her things for work.

"I popped by the Samba yesterday to see you," her mother went on. "But the manager said you'd already left. A darlin' man, though a tad too serious. And I told him he'd better treat my baby right."

Alyssa scrunched her eyelids closed. Her mother's mouth had always been set on "shoot to kill and ignore the questions later." Through the years, working in a country and western bar as a waitress had honed her manners to a sharp point, while Alyssa's business had necessitated softening the edges. And now Charles, Paulo's Chief of Operations, a man Alyssa hadn't even met yet, had been reprimanded by her mom.

Perfect.

With a quiet sigh, Alyssa reached for her keys. "Mom, please tell me you didn't."

"Oh, relax, Lyssa. He probably thought I was joking," her mother said. The whoosh of a melodramatic exhale came from the phone. "It's just this new job of yours makes me nervous."

Alyssa ignored her own doubts and tossed her keys into her purse. "Paulo Domingues already knows about my record."

"It ain't your record I'm worried about."

Of course not. Alyssa slowly shook her head, a baffled grin creeping up her mouth. Her mother's attitude never ceased to amaze her. "Mom, I was convicted of shoplifting." She set her purse on the table. *"Twice."*

"Oh, who cares about that?" her mother said with a dismissive tone, as if the arrests were irrelevant.

Alyssa gaped mutely at the cellular. Did she really think no one did? Then again, in the world according to Cherise Hunt reality was optional. As a matter of fact, it was often actively discouraged. Only fourteen years older than Alyssa, her brash personality was an eclectic combination of both soul sister and quirky parent, and Alyssa was never sure which role her mom would assume.

Her mother went on. "Between Paulo Domingues with his money and a hotel full of hoity-toity guests, well…" Her voice trailed off.

Alyssa gripped her phone with her hand. Was she worried her daughter would screw up again?

"I just don't want to see you get hurt, baby," her mom said.

The concern in her voice melted Alyssa's heart. As frustrating as her mother sometimes was, as many mistakes as she'd made, it had always been the two of them against the world. She'd taught Alyssa how to skirt a security camera, and she'd fought tooth and nail to keep their two-person family going during some desperate, destitute years. Alyssa owed her everything. And, while her mom sometimes made things more difficult, she always meant well.

Alyssa's tone grew soft. "I won't get hurt."

"Good. Because watching those highfalutin' college classmates of yours treat you like dirt near broke my heart."

Alyssa's fingers clamped harder around her cellular as a self-directed slap of anger surged. "Things are different now."

She was different now.

No longer was she the delinquent eighteen-year-old who'd believed people would give her a second chance after her first conviction. And although the narrow-minded behavior was always disappointing, it never surprised her anymore. Which was why she still couldn't wrap her brain around the fact Paulo hadn't fired her. Did he really not mind, or was he just stringing her along, waiting for a more opportune moment to lower the boom?

Confused, Alyssa dropped into a chair at her dining room table. "I've got to get ready for work, Mom."

"Good luck, baby. I'll bring you dinner tonight to celebrate your fancy new account."

Alyssa signed off and set her cellular aside, staring at her computer on the dining room table. Maybe it was a bit premature to be celebrating.

Because, no matter how hard Alyssa tried, she couldn't shake the thought Paulo still might use her past against her. It didn't seem the sort of thing he would do, but she'd learned long ago to never take anything for granted. It was one of many luxuries she couldn't afford. And arming herself with knowledge via a friendly bout of internet searching couldn't hurt.

After powering up her laptop, Alyssa tapped Paulo's name into the keyboard and hit Enter, dismayed by the list that popped onto the screen. The number of entries was so large she could read for a month and never reach the end. Apparently it wasn't just his star factor as the industry's cutting edge, unorthodox entrepreneur that made him hugely newsworthy.

Frowning, she typed in Paulo's name and "Domingues International Resorts," and another long list of articles was displayed. She scrolled through several screens until one from a local tabloid instantly caught her eye.

Paulo Domingues Ditched by Wife for Brother.

The headline punched with a powerful force.

Damn. Alyssa sat back and stared at the screen. She wanted

a little dirt on the man, a tidbit to throw back in his face should he decide to investigate her further. But this kind of news was too low for her to use. No one should have something so despicable and painful wielded as ammunition against them. Her eyes dropped to the next headline.

Local Hotel Magnate Removed from Country Club by Police.

Now she was getting somewhere.

This one was on the same date as the caption above, and she doubted it was a coincidence. Unable to stop the snooping about his breakup now, she clicked on the article and began to read.

At lunchtime, Paulo made his way into the empty hotel parking garage. The sun was scorching, and the sidewalk along Ocean Drive was full of female tourists in short shorts and midriff-baring tops. But his mind was stuck on a bland suit filled with the luscious body of Alyssa Hunt.

He hadn't stopped by to see her yet today, wanting to delay their meeting until he felt more in control. The makeout session yesterday had left an indelible heat that couldn't be washed away with a hundred cold showers. Paulo was still steaming from that one, chock-full-of-trouble kiss. He'd spent a good part of his morning being interrupted by fantasies starring Alyssa. Most of them involved him entering her office, hoisting her onto the desk, and taking her, right then and there.

Man, he was slipping.

With a grunt of disgust, he threw his leg over the back of his motorcycle. His frown grew deeper when he heard Alyssa's voice.

"I learned a few things about you today," she said.

Paulo looked up and watched her approach, her heels tapping on the concrete, the sound echoing off the walls. But it was the sight of her prim navy pantsuit that wiped the frown from his face, because he'd learned something, too.

Alyssa was all passion, kept tightly contained within a package of sassy Southern priss.

But that didn't mean he should linger in her company. He reached for the helmet hanging from the handle of the Ducati. "What did you learn?"

"Apparently you've had a run-in with the law yourself."

He froze in the midst of lifting his headgear, and slowly lowered his hands back down. "Decided to do a little research to get even?"

"Not to get even. That would be petty." She came to a halt beside the bike. "I figured it was only fair I knew more about you."

She would. And it amused him. "And did you succeed?"

"I guess I was busier the first year of my business than I thought. I missed out on quite a few stories about you in the local newspapers five years ago. Several in the *Miami Insider*."

The amusement instantly died. Leaning back, he schooled his face into an easy expression. "Don't believe everything you read. Journalists like to embellish. Especially ones at that tabloid." He shrugged easily, as if the topic didn't disturb him. "Conflict sells. That's why I don't answer reporters' questions."

"Never?"

With a growing need to escape, he pushed the start button, and the Ducati came to life with a purr. "Never."

She raised her voice over the idling bike, the purring sound reverberating in the deserted parking garage. "I just have one thing I want to ask."

Staring at her, he considered driving off. He'd spent a whole year of his life fielding questions about that day. Being chased by the paparazzi. Journalists camped out, waiting for him to walk by. Pouncing as soon as he appeared. The only safe havens had been home and Nick's club, but that was only because Security there had been trained to recognize every reporter in town and toss them out the door.

And hell if he'd start answering questions now.

Hoping to knock her off course, he sent her a scorching look, his gaze sweeping down her pristine suit to her designer shoes and back up, lingering along the way. By the end, he was wound tight again. And he wondered if the look got her as worked up as it did him. "I'll answer your question right after you drive this motorcycle."

Her hesitation was incredibly brief. "Deal."

Paulo slowly raised his brows. There seemed no end to the ways this woman would surprise him. She'd called his bluff again. And, as usual, he was too captivated to resist. He shut off the motorcycle, the silence vibrating around them.

His statement came out as more of a question. "You're going to drive the Ducati."

"After you show me how."

He bit back the smile. "I didn't realize that was part of the conditions."

"It is now." A fleeting look of concern crossed her face. "And I have one more. No kiss."

He allowed a small grin to lift the corner of his lips. On that subject they were in perfect agreement. "Absolutely no kiss." He crossed his arms, eager to see how she'd pull off driving his motorcycle. No doubt with her pinky lifted, as if holding a delicate cup of tea, all the while cussing under her breath. "So what's the question?"

"Is it true the police were called to kick you out of the country club?" she said. "For fighting with your brother?"

The mention of Marcos skidded helter-skelter down his spine, leaving skidmarks of anger along the way. He sent her an indifferent look. "It wasn't like I was arrested."

She colored slightly and scowled at him. "You caught a break because of your wealth."

"Maybe. But it wasn't my fight that got me thrown out."

"So why did they boot you out the door?"

His answer came out smooth, but only because he'd had a year of practice giving it. "I got kicked out because I refused to put on a coat and tie." He shrugged. "Too bad, too. Missed out on a good meal of lobster and prime rib."

She stared at him, her gaze scanning his face, as if looking for more beneath his expression. "That's what you told the *Miami Insider* reporter." She placed a hand on her hip and looked unconvinced. "So it had nothing to do with the fact you'd just learned your wife left you for your brother?"

He hadn't been left. He'd been *played*.

The bitterness went deep, leaving a wide gash. And the festering wound refused to heal.

Strung out from his years on the fast track at Domingues International, he'd thought a little easy company at the end of a long day would be nice. A union with a childhood friend, his father's goddaughter, a woman who understood the family and its dedication to the business, had seemed smart.

In retrospect, it had been anything but.

Three months after exchanging vows with Bianca in a simple ceremony, Paulo had known it had been a mistake. And even though they'd started out caring for each other, he'd been miserable. She'd been miserable. And the affection had started to wane. But he'd stuck it out because he'd made a promise. And if Bianca had simply asked for a divorce because it wasn't working, because he refused to conform to her tastes in clothes or behavior, he'd have chalked it up as a learning experience and moved on. Instead, she'd walked out when he had threatened to leave Domingues International and hooked up with the man who inherited the company. His *brother*. It was then that Paulo had finally realized the truth.

Bianca had wanted the Domingues name, the money and all the status that came with it.

Resentment burned his gut, leaving another black mark on his soul.

He forced an easy expression on his face. "Nope, the country club incident had nothing to do with her leaving. Marcos and Bianca are welcome to each other." Made for each other, more like it. Paulo hadn't talked to either of them since. No point.

Alyssa's face softened. "I don't think you really mean that."

"You're free to believe whatever you want."

For the first time, she looked unsure of herself. "For what it's worth...I'm sorry."

Her expression was so honest he almost believed she was concerned he'd been betrayed. That the only family he'd ever had that cared—his wife—had walked out on him. Turned out her affection was all an act.

His gut burned from the memory. "Nothing to be sorry about."

"Is that why you left Domingues International when your father died?" she asked.

Another flicker of emotion came and went inside—this one just as strong, just as intense—but he locked it up tight before it could fully escape. "You used up your one question." He kept his hands on the handlebars as he dismounted, holding the bike upright. "Time for the lesson."

She glanced at the Ducati, a worried look creeping up her face. "Before we get started, can you explain why people who live in a state known for its tropical storms choose transportation without doors and roofs, seatbelts for safety..." Her voice died out as she looked down at her dress pants and then back at the motorcycle. "Not to mention regular seats to maintain your dignity?"

After glancing around the deserted garage, Paulo sent her a wry look. "I know it will be difficult for you, but there's no one here you need to impress." The frown on her face grew bigger as she eyed the motorcycle, and he had to suppress the grin. "Are you going to back out?"

Her shoulders snapped back. "Of course not."

This woman seemed incapable of backing down from a challenge. And he was starting to enjoy himself now. The look on her face was almost worth the miserable trip down memory lane. "Why don't you take a sec to get a feel for her?"

"Her?" Alyssa blew out a breath and stared at the motorcycle, feeling foolish. What about this monstrosity made it female? And why in God's name had she agreed to this plan?

She knew why. Paulo and his exasperating mix of male magnetism and good looks. The more she learned, the more she wanted to know about the man. And his blithe treatment of his family's actions was astonishing. Not once had she seen a sign the conversation disturbed him. The laid-back, carefree attitude was firmly intact.

And, dangerous as it was, she had to admit she enjoyed his company.

But the amused look in his eyes couldn't be ignored. She wiped a damp palm down her pants. Finally giving in, she gingerly threw a leg over the bike and gripped the handles.

With a little more of a wiggle, she sat back on the seat. "*She* feels fine." Alyssa glanced down at the hard concrete, and her stomach twisted with fear. "I'm not so sure I do, though."

"Trust me. You're going to love it."

"I'll admit I enjoyed the ride yesterday." What little she remembered beyond touching him included the wind whipping by, the salty ocean air, and the bright sunshine on her skin. There was a sense of freedom that she hadn't anticipated. "But driving one…?"

One hand on the handlebar, Paulo leaned closer. "Afraid?"

Her heart began to misbehave at his proximity and the *café con leche* eyes. This time she told the truth. "Yes." She kept her voice even, resisting the urge to look at his mouth. "Especially of exotic-looking ones that are worth a bazillion dollars."

He tipped his head quizzically, his eyes crinkling with a curious humor. "Are we still talking about my motorcycle?"

A warm flush filled her stomach. "Of course." She cleared her throat. "I wouldn't want to ruin her."

A wry smile twisted on his lips. "Excellent point." Paulo threw his leg over the seat behind her and, like a slice of green tomato dropped in boiling oil, her nerves came to life with a sizzle.

Well...*hello*. This wouldn't help her concentration any.

Her back was pressed against his chest, her hips sandwiched between his thighs. She gripped the handles of the Ducati, her knuckles turning white. And maybe her dignity wasn't the most important thing she had to lose right now. Maybe it was her mind.

Neither of them moved for a moment. Being wrapped in Paulo's lean form was an odd combo of security and danger, and Alyssa's confused senses couldn't decide which she liked better.

"I never fully appreciated the motorcycle as a sexual symbol before," he murmured, his mouth at her ear. Paulo turned his head, nose at her neck, and inhaled. Her breath caught as goosebumps pricked her skin, and the fiery heat left her feeling oddly damp all over. "Now I do."

"Paulo..." The protest died when he placed his hands on her thighs and her mouth lost the ability to articulate.

"Don't worry." The rumble of his voice was at her ear. "I'm only here to keep the bike from falling over on you while you learn. I'll keep my promise. No kiss."

Shoot, who needed a mouth when hard muscle enveloped you like a second skin? In hindsight, it seemed a worthless condition. And how the heck was she supposed to follow his instructions now?

But the longer she sat frozen in place, the longer she'd be subjected to this torture.

Ignoring her body's chaotic response, she followed Paulo's directions and started the engine, easing the lever out. The bike crept forward. The minor accomplishment fueled her courage, and she grew more daring, gingerly twisting the throttle to pick up speed.

Over the next thirty minutes Alyssa managed to survive the distraction of Paulo's hands on her thighs *and* several trips around the first level of the garage. With each pass, the triumphant feeling grew stronger until, finally, she ventured to the top of the building and back. By the time she came to a stop on the ground floor, she didn't bother to contain her excitement.

Alyssa turned in the seat to flash Paulo a smile, her words a heavy drawl. "That was fantastic."

The smile died the moment she met his gaze, inches from hers. Thick lashes framed hazel eyes that glowed with an intensity hot enough to burn a hole in the ozone layer. There was no grin. No shared amusement. His hands scalded her through her pants. And the sight of his sensual lips, so close to hers, had the blood howling in her veins.

And suddenly Alyssa was sorry she'd made him promise not to kiss her. Because she longed to taste him again. To feel those large hands touch her between the legs. She shifted her hips, hoping to end the agony, only to wind up pressing her backside against his hard erection. Streaks of white-hot desire blazed, and she nearly groaned out loud.

His hand slid higher on her thighs, holding her hips in place, his voice husky. "If you don't want me to kiss you, you shouldn't look at me like that."

Heart pounding like a bass drum, Alyssa stared at him. Long denied, pent up desire demanded to be satisfied, and need finally overruled her good sense. "Maybe I've reconsidered my condition."

Several beats passed before he narrowed his eyes a fraction, gaze lingering on her mouth, as if considering her blatant offer. "No," he said softly, and her heart dropped at the word.

"I made a promise, and I intend to keep it." And with that, he dismounted.

Dazed, every cell punch-drunk with the buzz of desire, she stared at him.

Paulo looked down at her. "I think you should go to lunch." He leaned forward to unhook his helmet from the back of the bike, his face achingly close to hers. "Before I change my mind."

She gripped the handles hard, fighting the urge to close the distance between their lips. But pride drove her chin higher. "Who's to say I won't change *my* mind?"

He flashed her a deliberate look, as if he knew all her secrets. "We both know you won't."

CHAPTER FOUR

THAT was it. No more trying to get the upper hand, or any other part of her anatomy, on Paulo Domingues.

Alyssa sat at an outdoor café, ignoring the patrons droning on around her and shredding her napkin, alarmed on so many levels her mind spun from the turmoil. Down the street, the gorgeous gold marquee of the Samba glistened in the sunshine. She'd needed to get away, because eating lunch at her desk wasn't conducive to recovery.

The kiss at the park obviously hadn't been an aberration, and she didn't trust herself around the man anymore. It wasn't that she had—in a roundabout way, anyway—just asked her client for a kiss. It was worse than that.

The horribly, terribly, awful part was she'd practically *begged* him for it.

And not only with her words, she knew. She had begged in every possible manner. With her tone. Her gaze. In the way her body had leaned, *screaming* in its intent, closer to his.

She planted her elbows on the glass tabletop and groaned, dropping her face to her hands. No one could miss that blatant a come-on. And then, with desire etched in her every attitude…

He'd turned her down.

The turbulent chaos in her body intensified as she relived the sharp stab of longing followed by the crash of disappointment.

After the vow she'd insisted he take, she had shamelessly encouraged him.

How could she be so dumb?

In college, when rumors about her arrest in high school began to circulate, the effect had been swift and immediate. Labels had been attached to her faster than a game of pin the tail on the donkey.

Because if she was a thief, she must be easy too, right?

And, though the rumors weren't true, that hadn't stopped her classmates from indulging in a bit of fun, the stories growing more elaborate as they were passed along.

Alyssa rubbed her overheated cheeks. So what must Paulo think of her?

She'd set out to secure the account at the Samba, and then let the world's hottest hottie muck up her priorities. Outmaneuvering him might have been fun. It might have felt good. But letting down her guard and burning it up with him between the sheets wasn't going to impress Paulo.

Work. That was how she needed to impress the man. She was good at her job. *Excelled* at it. She needed to show him what she could do.

Feeling better now that she had rescrewed her head on right, she checked her phone. An email from the caterer doing the grand opening blinked on screen, reminding her about their meeting tomorrow morning to discuss the layout for the buffet. Alyssa picked up her fork and dug into her pasta salad, gazing at the message.

But, no matter how hard she worked on the last minute details of the opening, it was still someone else's creation. She needed to solicit a new client for the Samba. And not just any event. It had to be something amazingly spectacular. Something that allowed her the creative freedom to produce a dazzling party that showcased her talent.

And she didn't have much time.

She had to get Paulo to give up this need for a supervisory role. Because if she spent many more days in "daily direct contact" with him, who knew what she'd do next?

The following afternoon Paulo entered the lobby of the Samba and grabbed a bottle of water from the refrigerator behind the bar. The sound of the rock waterfall backdrop failed to calm the pulsating memory of yesterday's ride with Alyssa.

The lilac scent of her neck.

Her hips, firmly pressed between his thighs.

After twisting the cap off the plastic, he slugged back an icy sip to ease the churn of desire, his gaze drifting across the lobby to the staff hallway. Alyssa's first no-holds-barred smile from the day before was forever branded in his brain. And her look of unleashed desire? That particular expression had kept him up last night. Refusing to kiss her had been tough, but he wanted to prove to himself that he could.

The only thing walking away had proved was that he was deep in denial.

Their relationship was past the point of no return. She wanted him as much as he wanted her. And the more he fought it, the more securely he was caught in the web of attraction. Now the only way out he could see was to take it to its predictable conclusion. In bed with Alyssa. A few nights spent with her in his arms would free him to move beyond this frustrating fixation.

The familiar tap of heels on hardwood caught his attention, and he turned to see Alyssa crossing in his direction. Fresh, lovely, and bound up tight in a silk blouse and skirt. All he wanted was to strip the fabric away and discover the body beneath.

He rounded the bar. "Ready for another lesson?"

She came to a halt beside him, looking uneasy. "I don't think I'll ever be ready."

He was beyond ready.

Paulo propped his foot on the rung of a stainless steel barstool. At least she wasn't freezing him out with her professional face. Definitely progress. "It's not unusual to be a little apprehensive at first."

"I'm not apprehensive."

"Seemed that way yesterday." His tone shifted lower. "Until the end, anyway."

She ignored the innuendo and climbed onto a seat, primly crossing her legs.

Was she sending him a message?

"I have a more important matter to discuss," she said. "The caterer for the grand opening told me the pipes burst in the Twin Palms' ballroom today."

He shrugged. "That's the price one pays for working with historic hotels."

"Yes, well, it's left Rachel Meyer without a venue for her wedding reception."

She waited, as if this were something that affected his life. Other than feeling sorry for the engaged woman, who clearly lacked good sense, it was nothing to him.

Alyssa went on. "She's a best actress nominee for that indie film she did last year."

"I know who she is."

"She's a hot commodity in Hollywood right now, so her wedding is sure to generate terrific coverage."

Looking nervous, she touched the tip of her pink tongue to her lower lip, and the sight tackled his libido and pinned it to the ground. Maybe yesterday's fantasy should be adjusted. Her desk would be good, but if he pushed up her skirt even a barstool—

"The reception is two nights before our official opening, but I want to go after the account," she said.

His eyes still fixated on her mouth, the racy vision of the two of them dispersed with a pop.

She wanted to *what*?

Staring at her, he slowly lowered his foot to the floor. Long ago, when he'd still worked for Domingues International, he'd fought with his brother over the viability of the Samba. Marcos had wanted to sell it. Paulo had wanted to reinvent it.

His brother had eventually won.

And when Paulo had finally set out on his own business venture, every hotel he'd bought and turned into a prosperous enterprise, every dollar he'd earned, had been to guarantee that—if the Samba came up for sale again—he was ready to prove Marcos wrong. Now he was close to unveiling his vision, and she wanted to risk a catastrophe before they even opened?

"I realize the situation is a little unusual," she said, smoothing a silky strand of hair behind her ear. "But it's an opportunity to really market the Samba."

He couldn't decide whether to strip off her clothes and make love to her or send her to have her head examined. Instead, he gripped his bottle. "Or splash a very public nightmare across the papers if it's a disaster."

She didn't look discouraged. "It wouldn't be a disaster."

"And you know this *how*?"

Alyssa drew herself up to her full height. "Because I'll be in charge of it."

"It's only fourteen days away."

She opened her mouth, most likely to argue, when his Chief of Operations greeted them as he approached, saving her from herself.

When the man stopped beside him, Paulo kept his eyes on his overzealous, perplexing event planner and made the introductions. "Charles, this is Ms. Hunt. Alyssa, this is Charles Belvidere, my right-hand man."

The manager turned to Alyssa, and instantly she felt like a bug under a magnifying glass. Middle-aged, slim, with streaks of silver in his dark hair, he was tall. Distinguished. Between his black suit and his staid nature, he exuded the aura of a funeral director.

"Ah, yes," he said, his face was solemn. "I met your mother."

Her mouth went dry. It was obvious he had something more to say.

"She's quite…" Charles paused, as if searching for just the right word.

Alyssa didn't have an English degree, but she was pretty sure such a word didn't exist. With a small sigh, she rested her elbow on the counter, knowing this could take a while.

"Distinctive," Charles finally finished.

She added "politically correct" to her list describing the manager.

"Alyssa wants to go after the Myer reception," Paulo said.

Irked by his tone, she shot Paulo a frown. Both men were looking at her as if she'd declared she wanted to organize the inaugural ball for the President.

Charles adjusted the wire-frame glasses on his nose, looking uncomfortable. "I'll leave you two to your discussion."

She watched Charles walk away and then turned back to Paulo, prepared to resume the debate. "I'm quite capable of handling this job."

"You have no experience with an event of this size, and there's not enough time."

"Everything for the reception is in place. There's plenty of staff to help." She held his gaze, feeling less then steady despite her tone. He hadn't been this worked up during the conversation about his wife. His red T-shirt hugged the muscles beneath and, combined with the well-worn jeans, fostered a James Dean look. But this rebel most definitely had a cause. And its name was the Samba. "They just need a new venue," she added.

A few beats passed as his eyes slowly narrowed to questioning slits. "Did you have anything to do with the pipe incident at the Twin Palms?"

She rolled her eyes. "Oh, for goodness' sake."

"No strategic sabotage?" Her cheeks flamed as he went on. "Or convenient accident?"

Alyssa forced her chin to remain level. "I'm not going to dignify that with a response."

He waited a moment before going on. "Well, unless your days consist of more than the usual twenty-four hours, how are you going to pull this off in two weeks? *And* deal with the last-minute details of the grand opening?"

"I'll manage." Of course it wasn't quite as easy as she'd made it out to be, but she wasn't afraid of hard work. He simply stared at her, and she exhaled with a force that matched her frustration. "I'm *tryin'* to do the job you hired me for."

"Yes." He set his water bottle on the bar and sent her a grim look overflowing with doubt. "A job I'm not entirely convinced you're ready to do," he finished softly.

Alyssa's heart slowed to a dull thud. He didn't think she could do it.

That was what this was all about. He simply believed she wasn't capable.

As the depressing thought settled deeper, her chest grew tight. When he'd kept her on, despite her record, she'd thought it signaled he had some respect for her abilities. That all those events listed on her résumé—the ones she'd sacrificed so much to organize—counted for something. *Meant* something. But, when push came to shove, they didn't matter enough. And his doubt hurt, because the one thing she was absolutely sure of in her life was her skill as an event planner.

And to think she'd almost begged this man for a kiss.

"You don't trust me," she said.

He paused before replying. "This is business. It isn't personal."

The words cut off her breath in her throat. It was personal

when your work was all you had. "It would be foolish to pass on this opportunity," she insisted.

His face shifted through a sequence of emotions until it landed on resigned agreement. "You're right." He stepped closer, and her heart responded to his proximity, though his reluctant tone did little to repair her wounded pride. "But let me make myself clear." His frown grew deeper. "You're not to make a single decision without checking with me first. I want to know what you're doing every step of the way. And I expect detailed daily reports on your progress."

Breathing hard, she met his gaze. He wanted reports? She'd give him reports. Squaring her shoulders, she said, "Not a problem."

Feeling the need to flee, she turned and headed for her office. Hand in a fist, her palm was damp. And not just from nerves.

He pushed her sensual buttons just by entering a room, torching her blood and leaving her in flames. When she'd come out of her office and seen him across the lobby it hadn't mattered how many lectures she'd given herself, every cell in her body had done a happy dance. How could she have the hots for a man who didn't respect her work?

Her whole life was wrapped up in her business.

Her nails bit into her palm. Okay, so she would show him just how good she was. He'd never doubt her again. And she would enjoy watching him eat the crow she served him.

Once Alyssa had sold the bride-to-be on relocating her displaced event to the Samba, the two weeks passed in a flurry of activity. On the surface, Paulo had managed to keep his interactions with Alyssa strictly businesslike. Their daily meetings, complete with printed reports rivaling the size of the Dade County phonebook, had been brief.

Because Alyssa never stood still for long, working nonstop.

This morning the hotel had been crawling with temporary

hires hustling to produce today's miracle. And directing the chaos, calm and in control, had been Alyssa with her phone… displaying the to-do list that consumed her life.

A to-do list that had served its purpose well, because tonight the reception had gone down without a hitch. And now his concern wasn't that she couldn't do her job, it was that perhaps she did it *too* well.

At first he'd been pleased with how hard she worked, but as the days wore on watching her slowly kill herself organizing this event had had him rethinking his opinion. So did the exhaustion in her face. No one should work that hard. Ever. Especially when someone else reaped the majority of the awards.

Namely…him.

Disturbed, Paulo frowned as he rode the elevator to the top of the Samba. Not satisfied with merely shifting the arranged event to his empty hotel, Alyssa had set out to exceed the bride's previous expectations. Guests had lingered in the lobby, enjoying cocktails from the waterfall bar, before moving on to dinner in the reception hall. But by far her greatest coup had been the dance area she had created from scratch on the rooftop deck.

Paulo exited the elevator and took in her efforts. Hurricane candelabrums lined the railing, while floating candles adorned with white orchids drifted in the pool, casting a gentle light into the nighttime sky. Low sectional couches of dark mahogany and white cushions were arranged in cozy groups, emulating a trendy nightclub. An ethereal gazebo of draping swaths of white fabric made up the temporary dance floor.

And now that the last guest had finally left the building he needed to find the woman who was driven to perfection at her business.

He spied Alyssa standing at the far rail and, like a cell phone set on vibrate, his body hummed with awareness.

In the days since their disagreement, every night had been filled with dreams of her. And every morning he opened his eyes to find his body tangled in the sheets, soaked with sweat and burning for Alyssa.

The multitude of tasks she'd had to accomplish for tonight, every one of which he'd overseen, had thrown them into constant contact. Alyssa had gone back to pretending the attraction didn't exist. But with every activity the underlying sexual tension between the two of them had climbed higher and higher. Until he'd thought he'd spontaneously combust.

Paulo studied her. In her standard suit and pumps, she radiated confident professionalism, but she was so much more than that. Now his need for her was about more than putting out the fire and ending his preoccupation. He wanted Alyssa to learn to release her passionate side. To immerse her in the kind of pleasure that would remind her she was a beautiful, sensual woman.

With mounting expectation, he approached her. Alyssa's face glowed from the flickering candlelight and the neon lights of South Beach beyond. Her black jacket was tailored, but a slip of silk peeked from beneath.

"Are you ready to kiss and make up?" he asked.

"That would turn this personal," she said coolly.

He resisted the urge to smile. "You're still mad at me."

"More like disappointed."

He leaned an elbow on the rail. Dishes clinked in the distance as the staff gathered dirty cocktail glasses, bustling to clean up the aftermath. "I'll admit I had serious reservations about your abilities. But never let it be said I can't admit to being wrong. And as for the kiss during your motorcycle lesson…" A fleeting look of desire crossed her face, only to be replaced by one of embarrassment, and he leaned close, hoping to bring the first expression back. "On that issue, I concede to your wisdom, too."

Staring at him, she tipped her head. "Have you considered you might be overestimating your charms?"

His smile finally won. "It's high time we give in to the inevitable." To bring his point home, he brushed a strand of hair from her cheek, savoring the smoothness. "I already have." Her eyes went from silver to slate, and fierce need slammed into him with the force of a head-on collision, killing his grin.

Hell. He was right back where they'd left off the day of their ride.

Hard. Wanting her.

By now her poise was back in place. "Nothing is inevitable," she said. But despite the words her protest sounded thin, and there was a husky quality to her tone. "And don't you have better things to do than monitor every move your event planner makes?"

"Monitoring my event planner's moves has become a favorite pastime of mine."

"Yes," Alyssa said dryly. "And I can't figure out how you've managed to build a thriving enterprise with priorities like that."

Paulo's lips quirked at her tone. As if success could only be achieved by those who bartered their soul to the devil along the way. Like the years he'd spent consumed by his job. He'd almost given up racing his motorcycle, and though Nick had always stopped by the office to see him Paulo had never once enjoyed the club he'd helped his friend finance. Not until he left Domingues International.

"I'm living proof you don't have to kill yourself to build a prosperous business," he said. And that was just one of many lessons he wanted to share. Starting tonight. "I worked hard for the last ten months, restoring the Samba, but I still found time for the things I enjoy." Doubt radiated from her face, and he lifted an eyebrow. Fun shouldn't be this hard to sell. "With the pace you keep, eventually you'll burn out. Something I learned firsthand."

"I've never seen you in a suit and tie. So I can't picture you as a burnt-out executive."

"Life's too short to spend it with a noose around your neck."

He let out a small scoff. "A concept my family never understood." Paulo gripped the metal rail with both hands, staring at the city lights and fighting the threatening return of bitter memories. "I don't do suits and ties. Ever. But burnt-out executive I know well. Now..." He sent Alyssa a mock stern look. "Have a seat while I go find us a drink," he said, and then headed for the bar.

Alyssa stared after him, wondering how a man could look so dashing in simple dark pants and a navy dress shirt. Despite the hellish work schedule, she'd missed their earlier easy camaraderie. With a flutter of nervous anticipation, Alyssa settled onto a couch. One of the staff wandered by, snuffing out the candelabrums that lined the railing, slowly lengthening the shadows on the deck.

When Paulo returned with two champagne flutes, he handed one to Alyssa and sat down beside her, throwing her instantly on guard.

Hoping to keep a lighthearted atmosphere, Alyssa sent Paulo an assessing look. "I always pictured you more as a beer connoisseur. I'm surprised to see you drink champagne."

"I do, but only when forced."

His words made her smile. "Who's forcing you?"

"The situation," he said as he threw his arm along the back of the couch. And though he didn't touch her, the potential was hard to ignore. He raised his drink between them. "To South Miami Beach's event of the year, and Elite Events for making it possible." Paulo tipped his flute against hers, and the delicate ting of crystal on crystal rang in the air. "Seriously," he said, his face reflecting his words, "you did an amazing job."

The sincerity in his tone floored her—one of those moments of candor that knocked her off her feet, affecting her as powerfully as his touch. Her smile melted away as warmth seeped into her heart. And it had nothing to do with the kind of heat Paulo usually excelled at creating. This kind seeped all the way to her soul. How could one man's words so effortlessly swing her from abject misery to unadulterated high? She was *supposed* to be gloating.

"Thank you," she said, surprised by the pressure of tears behind her lids.

Jeez, Alyssa. Blubber like an idiot, why don't you?

Feeling silly and overemotional, she sipped her bubbly champagne before continuing. "You worked hard, too."

And he had. Paulo had been there every step of the way, working alongside her. Wherever an extra set of hands had been needed, he'd rolled up his sleeves and pitched in. She'd learned that, despite his charm and piles of money, he was no slacker. Because when the linen vendor arrived late, and Alyssa had briefly panicked, it was Paulo who'd helped her spread the tablecloths on the dinner tables.

And the sexy billionaire hotelier surrounded by swaths of hot pink had been a sight to behold.

She shifted her gaze away from his, taking in the ambience. Dinner in the reception hall had been lovely, but the deck was her creation. Her baby. And throughout the evening she'd hovered behind the scenes, ensuring everything went smoothly, proudly watching from afar as the affluent crowd enjoyed her efforts.

To date, the most satisfying moment of her life.

Paulo set down his glass. "But I didn't come just to sing your praises." The only light now came from the candle on their coffee table. "I came to convince you to lift your embargo on men."

Her heart relocated to her throat and picked up its pace. Alyssa gripped her champagne glass, but didn't reply. Respect as colleagues was one thing, but a relationship was a more difficult can of worms. One she wasn't sure she wanted to open.

As her silence lingered, the side of Paulo's mouth twitched. "Last I checked, a vow of celibacy wasn't a requirement for an event planner. Wouldn't be much competition if it was. And the time to break that vow has come." Paulo shifted closer, his hard thigh pressing against hers. And the look he sent her lit her more effectively than if he'd doused her in brandy and set her ablaze. An Alyssa *flambé*.

Time for the close-to-the-bone truth.

She'd never wanted another man the way she wanted Paulo. Which was probably why it had been easy to give men a pass for a while…until now.

"I was hoping to start our new affiliation with a dance." Paulo glanced at the band members who were packing up their equipment. "I'm sorry I didn't get to salsa with you."

"I don't know how."

"Too bad. Because one of my prerequisites for involvement with a woman is the ability to salsa." The left corner of his mouth tipped up. "But in your case I'll make an exception."

Alyssa ignored the thrill of desire coursing through her veins. Obviously he had picked up on her weakening resistance and was feeling cocky. Too cocky. She worked hard for a deadpan face. "Am I supposed to be flattered?"

His dimple grew deeper. "Very."

Holding back the smile, Alyssa pursed her lips. "That's an interesting assortment of rules." She lifted her hand and ticked them off on her fingers. "No suits. No ties. No women who can't salsa." She arched an eyebrow, letting him know the last one was rip-roaringly ridiculous. "Any other additions to the list I should be aware of?"

"Only one more."

"And what's that?"

"No more engagement rings."

There was no mistaking the warning.

Paulo leaned closer, his eyes searching hers. "Is that a problem?"

His dark hair hung seductively to the side of his forehead, and his proximity sent her temperature spiraling, bringing memories of him wrapped around her on the Ducati. The rest of her body was busy remembering as well.

She stared back, breathing in his sandalwood cologne, knowing she'd regret it if she pushed him away. By the end of her motorcycle lesson, deep down she'd known the war within was over.

And she'd spent the last two weeks in Paulo's constant presence, thinking about the possibilities the entire time she'd been planning this event. Tormented by every accidental brush of his arm. Every brief touch of his hand. The occasional searing look. Until his simple presence robbed her of the ability to breathe. And finally she'd concluded she wanted to know, *had* to know, how it would be between them. The fact he'd stated up front it would be limited to a brief affair made it seem almost attainable.

Because did her past really matter if a permanent relationship wasn't part of the equation?

Rubbing the condensation on her glass, she finally replied, her words soft. "No. That's not a problem."

Eyes dark, he ran a finger down her neck, trailing flames as he went. "You're lucky I'm a patient man."

"Lucky?"

"Yes."

"You think highly of yourself, don't you?"

"I suppose." He laid his hand at the base of her throat, and the warmth it generated rivaled the effect of an entire bottle of champagne. "This morning, I almost dragged you out of the reception hall and back to the office."

Goosebumps pricked. She knew the exact moment he was referring to, but she sent him a false innocent look. "To discuss work?"

He leaned close, his mouth almost touching hers. "Nope." A light brush of his lips across hers evoked electrifying messages. "You see, I have this ongoing fantasy involving you, me..." he took her lips again, this time drinking deeply before pulling back a fraction "…and the top of that desk of yours."

Lips aching for more, the pulse in her neck throbbing beneath his hand, she swallowed hard. "And do I get any say in these fantasies?"

"Absolutely." The fire in his eyes set her belly blazing, and his hand slid lower, dipping under her jacket. "I'll let you tell me all about them in my room." Their gazes locked, and his fingers brushed the curve of her breast.

She slowly shook her head, quaking with need. "You'll *let* me?" Obviously the man required a little more humbling. With a deep breath, Alyssa stood, bringing a startled look to Paulo's face, and she bit back a grin. "I should check on the staff." Fingers trembling, she drained the last of her champagne, trying to appear nonchalant. "Besides, I think it would do you some good to wait a little longer." She sent him a small smile. "You know, heighten the anticipation a little."

He stared at her blankly, as if she was speaking Greek. "You gotta be kidding me."

His expression was priceless. Working hard to keep her composure, she enjoyed the sensation of power, and her smile got bigger. "Why, Mr. Domingues, where is that infamous patience of yours?"

His eyes narrowed with growing suspicion. "Is this some sort of payback?"

Chuckling, she leaned forward, bringing her lips within inches of his. "Of course." She raised a brow, dropping her gaze to his mouth and enjoying her effect on him way too much. "Afraid I'll change my mind?"

"Hell, yeah," Paulo growled back, his eyes black with desire.

"You should be." Alyssa straightened up and sent Paulo a coy look. "I'll come find you when I'm done."

CHAPTER FIVE

AS THE last of the staff left the building, Alyssa glanced at her watch.

Almost 1:00 a.m.

Fatigue settled in her chest like dead weight. The moving crew had hauled away the rental furniture, and she had just finished her survey of the reception room and was on her way to the pool for its final inspection. As she crossed the lobby, she wondered where Paulo had wandered off to.

Maybe he had given up on her and gone home. Disappointment rose at the thought. But as she entered the elevator footsteps sounded behind her. Alyssa looked up and caught Paulo's reflection in the mirrored wall.

Her fatigue vanished as the doors slid shut behind him, and the elevator waited patiently for someone to push a button. But patience was the furthest thing from her mind. Still keyed up from their earlier encounter, she was a conflicted mass of nerves and need. "Where are you taking me?"

"The first time?" Paulo's eyes held hers in the mirror as he stepped closer. "Here."

Her mind balked at the answer, but her body didn't care as it began a chant of encouragement. She stared at Paulo's reflection, and then at her suit, unsure what to do next. The coy feeling of control from before was long gone.

It had been fun.

It had also been an act.

He must have seen her concern. "No more thinking about your work." He lowered his mouth to nuzzle her neck. "Now it's just you and me." Nipping a path toward her jaw, each rake of his teeth made her sizzle. But the starkly vivid vision of them in the mirror was too much, so she tried to turn in his arms for a kiss.

He stopped her by pulling her flat against his muscular frame, his erection hard against her backside. Moisture flooded her panties, and her heart thudded harder, as if pumping blood to all those suddenly engorged parts of her body took extra work.

"I know what you want," he said at her ear. "And we'll get to that, I promise." His arms encircled her, his cheek level with hers, his dark hair tickling her face. "But first..." Holding her gaze in the mirror, he began to undo her jacket, winding her tighter with every release of a button. "I want you to see yourself as I do."

Though awash in a sea of longing, she blinked twice, suddenly petrified. She knew how the guys in college had seen her. As trashy. Cheap.

A guaranteed lay.

Shame churned her stomach. She'd been hit on repeatedly, and with as much delicacy as a freight train, while they'd tried to prove the rumors true.

"How do you see me?" she said hoarsely. She was almost afraid to hear.

With a grasp of her lapels, Paulo peeled her coat down her arms, the fabric falling to the floor. "I see a lady who wears a crisp business suit," he said.

Her nerve slipped lower as he released the catch on her skirt. With a push, it landed at her feet, leaving her in just her camisole and panties.

A wolfish grin appeared. "With a daring red thong beneath."

Daring. The frantic beat of her heart made the term kind of ridiculous.

"Not so daring if no one sees it," she said quietly.

"*I* see it." Hooking her panties with his thumbs, he dragged the scrap of lace past her hips. Once her thong joined her skirt, with her help, he lifted her camisole and tossed it aside. Eyes devouring her, the grin on his face died. And so did the last of her frayed nerves.

Paralyzed, Alyssa stared at her reflection. A woman about to engage in a sexual exploit in an *elevator.*

She felt bared. Stripped of her constricting clothes. But without them she wasn't the cool business owner. The competent careerwoman. Her suit, her identity—her armor—lay in a pile at her feet.

And the moment was so blatantly sensual, so highly charged, it was overwhelming. Sure she'd make a fool of herself, she turned her face away from her image, trying for a light tone. "I just see a naked lady."

Holding her chin, he gently turned her face toward the mirror again. "A very *sexy* lady," Paulo said.

Her nipples tightened, and she knew Paulo noticed by his voice.

"One capable of great passion," he murmured huskily.

Was she? Her usual insistence on darkened bedrooms sometimes left her satisfied. Kind of. Then again, it always afforded her some measure of cover. And protection. But this…?

He slid his hands down and around to the front of her thighs, her eyes growing wider as he went. Fingers threading through her curls, he brushed his thumb across her clitoris. As the pleasure pierced her, she gripped her cheek between her teeth, staring at the risqué vision of the two of them.

No man had ever watched her reaction, and the scrutiny heightened the anticipation. Made it more acute. Left her edgy. But it was almost too erotic. And when he brushed her again, shooting sparks down her limbs, her thigh muscles clinched reflexively. She *couldn't…*

"It's okay," Paulo said. "Relax and enjoy the moment."

The pounding in her chest hurt. "It's not so easy for me," she whispered.

"I'll take care of you," he said. "Just open your legs."

Her breath hitched at his words, and she instinctively parted her thighs. Eyes on her face, he slid two fingers between her wet folds, and her jaw went slack at the sweet pressure. His free hand cupped her breast, caressing the tip.

Her senses were keyed up. Wired. And those magical hands were strong, sure, and so adept she wanted to weep from the pleasure.

"More," he demanded.

Mesmerized by his touch, she did as told and spread her legs wider, finally letting him in. Allowing him complete access. Placing herself in his care. Never had she had a moment where the attention was so purely on *her* needs. Just the freedom to be. To feel.

And, dear God, did she feel.

Thumb stroking her nub, he took the ecstasy higher, until it was sweet torture. Every nerve-ending was eager. Every touch, smell, even the sound of their breathing was amplified. And he played her body until it hummed. As the delicious rhythm bombarded her with volley after volley of need, she clutched his wrist, mouth open, frozen, afraid if she moved she'd break the spell. But Paulo would have none of that.

"Stop holding back," he said roughly against her ear. "Take what you want."

"I can't."

"Yes." Paulo's gaze bored into hers as he increased the pressure of his thumb. "You can."

She choked back a cry of pleasure, and tentatively began to rock her hips in time with his hand.

It was too much and not enough, all at once. A flame of desire shot straight between her legs, where his thumb captured it and stroked it even higher. Every sensation built on the one before, magnifying it.

Until her need teetered so high, so precariously, it was frightening.

The bone-melting heat in his eyes and the building tension left her trembling, her knees shaky. Driving her into sensual oblivion while he watched. She couldn't look away, trapped by his gaze and their reflection in the mirror, Paulo's one hand between her thighs, the other on her breast. Lips parted, a gasp escaped her throat with every in-and-out slide of his fingers.

"Make some noise, Alyssa." His hazel eyes looked black. "Just let go."

And suddenly she was tired of holding back.

Tired of denying herself.

Releasing the last of her doubt, Alyssa groaned and lifted her arms to thread her fingers through his hair. Cheeks hot, hair damp at the nape of her neck, she arched her hips.

Her movements grew stronger. Desperate. Wanting more. Demanding more. Her consciousness slipped to a higher level, a new state where she existed outside herself. A state of bliss. Euphoria.

And the mirror contributed to the out of body experience. Paulo, eyes on hers, whispered shockingly explicit words of encouragement in her ear as her body, in sync with his, moved with complete abandon. Uninhibited. Wanton.

Until, with a burst of light, the orgasm finally hit. The pressure of pleasure exploded outward, shocking in its ferocity. Her muscles convulsed around him, driving her hips to a frantic pace, riding the waves as she repeatedly cried out his name, the loud words echoing in the small space.

The silence that followed was marred only by her labored

breaths. She closed her eyes and let go of his head. Every cell throbbed with each erratic thump of her heart.

"That was beautiful," Paulo said, kissing her damp temple. "*You* are beautiful."

She opened her eyes, still wrapped in Paulo's arms, her legs limp. If he let go, she would surely slump to the floor in a heap.

"Was it worth waiting for?" Paulo asked.

All she could manage was a whisper. "Yes." And then some.

Paulo looked at her with intense scrutiny. "Hmm. No snappy comeback. No sharp retort to keep my ego in line." A slight lift of his lips. "Little Alyssa must have been moved."

Moved? Good Lord, she'd been rocked to the core. Her muscles still ached from the force of her climax, as if she'd just spent the day running through deep sand. How was she going to make it to the hotel room now? "I don't think I *can* move."

Paulo chuckled as he released her. "No problem." He began to undo the buttons on his shirt. "You don't have to."

Doubt overcame her weakness, and she whipped around to face him. What was he planning now? "Aren't we going to a bed?" With a lift of an eyebrow, Paulo reached for the bottom button. Her voice sounded strangled. "But—"

The word died when he peeled off his shirt. His chest was lean. The abdomen taut. She stared up at him, the wave of need returning. Because she wanted him again. With a fierceness that was alarming. As if the most amazing orgasm she'd ever experienced wasn't enough. Paulo pulled a condom from his pocket and then pushed his pants and briefs to the floor, kicking them aside. Now he was gloriously naked, his erection in full view, and desire sent her heart rate soaring again. But *how*…?

When Alyssa glanced at the marble floor, the uncertainty in her face was adorable, and Paulo felt compelled to reassure her. His little event manager had so much to learn. "No hard floors, I promise." Staring at her, he rolled on the condom, fascinated by the pink tint to her cheeks. "We'll do this standing up."

Her color rose higher. "That's impossible."

Paulo stepped forward to cradle her breasts. "It absolutely is possible," he said softly.

He brushed his thumbs across her nipples, and her mouth opened with a groan, wiping away her doubtful look. Satisfied, Paulo took her lips, slaking his across hers. And hers were warm. Sweet. Passionate, and yet surprisingly submissive. The aggressive, take-charge attitude was replaced with an eagerness to follow his lead. And the sense of power was exhilarating.

The mating tongues filled his mind with the image of what he wanted. Paulo lifted one of her thighs, wrapping her leg around his waist. The tip of his erection nudged her, a very frustrating touch too high. Grasping her buttocks, he shifted her up.

She pulled her mouth from his, her chest heaving. "Paulo, I don't think this will work—"

Her words ended when he thrust inside, and they both went still, staring at each other.

She was hot. Wet.

And so, so tight.

Struggling for breath, senses reeling, he pressed his forehead to hers as he fought the urge to pound into her, the feeling violent. The self-induced, masochistic plan to concentrate purely on her pleasure, to immerse her in sensation, had backfired. Now his own need was so great he was afraid he would hurt her. Jaw clenched, hands on her buttocks, he pinned her against the mirror and began to gently rock his hips.

But with every dig deeper Paulo felt his greed grow.

With every thrust inside his tempo increased.

Until the buck of his hips was strong. Hard. He'd never get enough of her. He burned with the fire she lit in him. Cheeks flushed, her mouth slack in a silent cry, careening sounds of pleasure began to slip from her throat. He recognized the call. The sharp bite of her fingernails on his shoulders. She was close.

Unfortunately he was closer. He wanted her with him when

he peaked, to feel her shatter around him again. For some inexplicable reason, if she wasn't experiencing that same powerful force his release wouldn't be as satisfying.

One hand supporting her, he reached between her legs to caress her slick center. The tip of his index finger landed where his shaft stroked her body, and the sense of possession was so fierce he almost came.

Gritting his teeth, embedded deep inside her, he paused again, his heart pounding. And as he stared at her it hit him. This was about more than simple satisfaction. More than just moving beyond a frustrating obsession. He had advanced, and she had retreated. He had thrust, and she had parried.

But right now, in this moment and time, she was *his*.

He reached up to pull her hand from his shoulder and press it between them, his fingers on top of hers, so she could feel where they were joined. Alyssa inched her leg higher on his hip, offering him more. At her silent acknowledgment he began to move again. High on the double pleasure of knowing she was experiencing the taking of her body in two ways, not just one. Thrusting harder and harder between her legs. Demanding. Rough. Ruthless in his pursuit of their pleasure, pushing it higher.

And when Alyssa let out a cry that bounced off the walls, her body clenching, the sound of her letting go drove him wild.

The feel of her orgasm made him crazy.

And with a flash of blinding light he followed her into oblivion.

Two days later Alyssa stood at the end of the staff hallway, watching the sunshine stream through the arched floor-to-ceiling windows of the Samba lobby. The tinkle of stemware and murmur of conversation filled the room. In the corner, the band played soft Latin music. The grand opening was well underway. And Paulo, in khakis and a dress shirt, mingled with the guests, looking relaxed and at ease.

Alyssa was anything but.

Because she couldn't delay the inevitable any longer.

When Paulo had finished with her in the elevator, he'd carried her to the penthouse. And what had come next was stupefyingly unbelievable. Alyssa had eagerly followed along wherever he led her, over and over again, leaving her limp from the pleasure. It had been more than she could have imagined. Better than what she'd heard. But when she'd opened her eyes in the morning she'd been handed a major reality check.

She'd slept with a client. A man who had never asked her for a date. Heck, she didn't even know where he *lived.*

And as her gaze had roamed the dim hotel room, the heavy brocade curtains blocking the light, an uneasy feeling had welled inside. The penthouse bedroom was beautiful. Opulent. But coldly formal. Completely lacking in any reflection of Paulo's personality.

But the worst part had been, even after a long night in his arms, she was hungry for more.

She'd turned her gaze to his beautiful face as he slept peacefully, his long, muscular legs tangled in the sheets. And the craving to wake him by sliding her tongue up his thigh and taking him in her mouth had been strong. Shocking in its intensity. She'd stared at him, struck dumb and utterly, utterly aroused, lost in the daydream.

And tortured by what it would say about her.

She was *supposed* to be a professional. And her sleek, polished air was hard to maintain when holed up in a dark, impersonal hotel room, preparing to throw herself at a man like a naughty nymphomaniac.

With fumbling fingers she'd dressed and quietly slipped from the room. After changing into the spare outfit she kept at her office, she had found the hired crew and thrown herself into the middle of the cleaning frenzy to prepare for today. Frantic for some space to regain her equilibrium.

But there was no avoiding him now. Of course their first meeting would be easier if she knew whether they'd just had a one-night stand or if Paulo intended for it to happen again.

And what would she say if he did? Or if he didn't? And why couldn't she decide which was worse?

She bit the tip of her fingernail, hating the feeling of uncertainty her life was filled with of late. Normally she set her sights on a goal and pursued it with the determined focus of a pitbull on Ritalin. Sometimes to her own downfall, as her mother loved to remind her.

And then, as if conjured by her thoughts, she heard her mom call her name.

Alyssa turned to watch her mother approach. With her voluptuous figure brazenly accentuated in a suede skirt, fringed Western shirt, fancy boots and her best cowboy hat, Cherise Hunt looked like a middle-aged rodeo queen.

All she needed now was a sash emblazoned with the words "Alyssa's Mother."

After all these years Alyssa was used to her dramatic entrances, but this one was particularly spectacular. She held back a dry smile as her mom drew closer. "Nice outfit."

Cherise touched the bleached-blond bob beneath her hat. "Just keeping in touch with my roots."

Alyssa's brow rose in amusement. "You've never been on a horse in your life."

Her mother fluttered a hand. "Details, Lyssa." Her eyes swept around the room. "Fancy-shmancy little shindig you cooked up here." She looked Alyssa up and down, and her gaze lost a little of its luster. "But Lordy, hon, must you dress like a repressed virgin?"

The amusement choked and died as heat flooded Alyssa's

face. She took her mother's arm and steered her toward the staff hallway, away from the crowd. "Mom, please."

"Oh, for Pete's sake, Lyssa. No one is listening." She eyed Alyssa's black pantsuit critically. Granted, it was more conservative than usual. But after her night with Paulo it felt appropriate. Her mother, however, looked concerned. "You're not, are you?"

With a sigh of confusion, Alyssa felt obligated to ask, "Not what?"

"A virgin?"

"Mom." Alyssa stopped inside the doorway to the back hall, sweeping her hand toward the crowd. "Does this look like the appropriate place to discuss this?"

"You never want to discuss anything important with me."

"That's not true. I just prefer private discussions take place in *private*." Alyssa lowered her voice to a whisper. "And, just for the record, for some people celibacy is a legitimate lifestyle choice."

Her mother sniffed delicately. "Ridiculous. What's the point of a lifestyle without the life?"

Three days ago Alyssa would have had several ready responses. After her adventures with Paulo she had none.

"Ms. Hunt."

Alyssa chimed "yes" in unison with her mother, turning to face the crowd as Charles approached them. But he wasn't addressing her.

The manager, looking refined in a pinstripe suit, held out his elbow to her mom. "Would you like a tour of our facilities?"

Beaming up at him with all the subtlety of a spotlight, Cherise Hunt slipped her hand through his arm. "Well now, sugar, aren't you the sweetest thing?"

Alyssa winced at her mother's endearment.

"Ms. Hunt," Charles said, this time looking at Alyssa. "Mr. Domingues would like you to join him in greeting the guests."

Greeting the guests? Alyssa clutched the hallway doorjamb, staring after Charles as he led her mother away, and then switched her gaze to the growing crowd—a host of South Miami Beach's richest and most influential people. Nausea formed a rock in her stomach.

A little awkward post-sex meeting paled in comparison. So far Alyssa had been working the event in the background, making sure everything went according to plan. Truthfully, there wasn't much to do, but all that wealth accumulated in one room was too much to face.

This is what you wanted, Alyssa. This is what you've been working for.

Good God, what had she been thinking?

She pressed the heel of her palm to her forehead and gulped for air. After a few seconds she dropped her arm to her side, shaking her hands to release the tension.

Do it, girlfriend. Just go.

With a smile plastered on her face, she stepped across the threshold, scanning the crowd for an approachable-looking group. Then she spied Tessa Harrison, mother of an old college classmate and a wealthy woman with a majestic air, a bazillion dollars' worth of jewelry gracing her designer pantsuit. Alyssa's steps faltered as fragmented visions flashed in quick succession.

Being treated like a servant at a catering job in the woman's home. Her condescending attitude during a charity banquet Alyssa had worked. The mocking tone of her daughter at college. And then the procession of shame landed on the granddaddy memory of them all: the parent-student luncheon her sophomore year at Osten College...the party that had ended with Alyssa being hauled out in the hands of the police.

The second time in her life her outfit had ended up accessorized with a pair of handcuffs.

Her ears filled with a threatening buzz as her head grew light.

Her lips tingled. Sweat beaded at her temples. Jeez, maybe she should take a moment to collect herself.

Heart thumping in her chest, Alyssa spun on her heel and crossed back into the staff section, sliding her hand along the wall to steady her steps as she headed away from the crowd. When she reached the far end of the hallway, though tempted to keep going, she leaned against the exit door for support. She closed her eyes and dropped her head back, concentrating on the music drifting up from the lobby.

You knew this day would come. You knew it.

Footsteps padded up the hall and came to a stop in front of her. She recognized the cologne. Paulo's spicy scent was forever entrenched in her memory after a night in his arms.

Oh, good grief. Could this moment get any more complicated?

"Are you all right?" he asked.

She kept her lids closed. "I'll be fine," she said. "Just feeling a little…" Terrified? Horrified? As if she was the shining star in the *World's Lamest Losers* reality show? And she sure wasn't referring to weight loss. "Intimidated."

"Why?"

She drew in a deep breath. "I don't function well around the wealthy."

"They're just people like you," he said. There was no irritation in his tone, only a pragmatic reassurance. "No better. No worse."

Alyssa opened her eyes and Paulo stood before her, a plate of chocolate-covered strawberries in his hand, a line of concern between his brows.

She blinked several times, and after a moment her heart recovered a bit. "Next you'll be telling me to picture the guests in their underwear."

A smile tugged the corner of his mouth. "I'd prefer you picture *me* in my underwear. Or, better yet, while you're making the rounds around the room…" He leaned closer. "Picture me naked."

The sound of music faded as she looked into thickly fringed smoky eyes, the slanted cheeks framed by dark hair. Her heart threatened to make a comeback. "Not exactly the vision I need right now."

With a puckered brow, he searched hers eyes for a moment, and then he leaned back, holding out his dish. "Do you want to talk about it?"

Her laugh was harsh. "Not particularly."

His voice went quiet. "Is this about your arrest?"

As she stared at his troubled face, she realized she had to say something. By now he must think his event planner was a total basket case.

She lowered her gaze to the fruit on his plate, nausea rolling again, and gathered her courage. "In high school I got caught shoplifting and was referred to a youth diversion program. I was assigned a job with a caterer." A weak smile lifted her lips. "An excellent teacher and a great boss. She paid me way more than I was worth." She let out a small scoff. "Which was a godsend."

His frown grew deeper. "You needed the money?"

She briefly lifted her eyes to his. "We needed the money."

A space of several seconds ticked past, as if he was waiting for her to elaborate. But she wasn't about to.

After returning her gaze to his plate, she concentrated on selecting a strawberry, as if the fate of the not-so-free world depended on it. It made telling the story easier. "But the first catering event I worked after starting college was at the home of a student from my freshman English class. Her parents' anniversary, I think," she said with a frown, trying to remember. Not that it mattered. "In my initial pass around the room with a tray of appetizers, my classmate spilled her drink on my shoes." Alyssa remembered that part well. She finally picked a berry.

"Before the night was over two of the girl's friends had tipped their drinks onto my tray."

"Not a coincidence, I gather?"

"No. And unfortunately that night was just the beginning." Alyssa cautiously nibbled on the end of her strawberry before continuing. When her stomach didn't complain, she swallowed. "Most of my classmates ignored me. Some were superficially polite, but others…" Her attention drifted back toward the lobby. "Some of the others were offended that I'd sullied the hallowed ground of their precious school. And Tessa Harrison was just one of several parents at Osten College who felt that way."

The grimace on his face spoke volumes. "Osten College?"

She lifted a helpless shoulder. "My boss was chairman of their board of admissions and pulled several strings to get me in on a scholarship. I figured a prestigious school would look good on my résumé." She cleared her throat before going on. "Better than a criminal record, anyway."

With a thoughtful expression on his face, Paulo set his plate on a hall table and then turned back to her. "Tessa Harrison is a shrew with three ex-husbands, every one of whom left her for a younger woman. Just remember that if you bump into her out in my lobby."

She shot him a grateful smile. His attempt to reassure her was sweet. Not exactly a word she would have associated with the man. But the thought of bumping into the woman had her stomach considering issuing a rejection slip to its contents. Alyssa pitched the rest of the strawberry into a nearby trash can and rubbed her temple, hoping he wouldn't notice the tremble in her fingers. "I'm not sure I can go out there."

He placed a hand on the door beside her head. Alyssa's heart rate skyrocketed as he ran a finger down her cheek, staring at her lips. Desire battled fear for her attention, and as the moment lingered desire began to win out.

She swallowed hard. "Aren't you tired of your event manag—?"

His mouth landed on hers.

Her body trained from their night together, Alyssa reacted immediately. The last vestige of her panic gave way to a monsoon of need. Opening her mouth for his tongue, she let his lips take hers as a hard thigh pressed against her intimately, and she arched against him, a sigh escaping her throat.

She was back in his arms again, and for one shining moment she forgot everything. The people in the lobby. Her past. All that was important was this man and the all-consuming power he had over her body. The kiss lingered until bells of warning rang in her head, signaling the need for air, and Paulo finally lifted his head.

"Yes, you *can* go out there." His breathing was ragged, and a twinkle appeared in his eyes. "And, no, I *won't* be tiring of the delicious challenge you present anytime soon."

Looking up at him, her heart battering away, Alyssa arched an eyebrow, trying her best to appear calm as the blood throbbed in her veins. She hadn't exactly fought his kiss. "Not much of a challenge anymore."

"I disagree. After an amazing night, I woke up alone."

Amazing night, indeed. And the noises that had come from her mouth…

Flushing at the memory, she fought to regain her composure. "I needed to supervise the cleaning crew."

"No," Paulo said, shaking his head. "I'm not buying it. You're just not used to the morning-after scene." He cocked his head. "You know how I knew?"

"I think we both know how. But I'm sure you're dying to tell me anyway."

"With every orgasm you had such a look of surprise."

She turned her face away, gnawing on her cheek. She'd wanted to know what sex with Paulo would be like, and now she did. Unfortunately she hadn't counted on getting such a delicious taste of what she'd been missing all these years. "I never knew they came in so many…flavors." Feeling ridiculous, she let out an embarrassed laugh.

He looked at her curiously. "Do you regret sleeping with me?"

She stared at him. Ever since she'd made him an exception to her rule, she had been putting herself through an emotional wringer. Unable to decide how she felt. Waffling between dismay and total delight. But, whatever happened next, he deserved an honest answer. She might question the future, left to muddle her way through unfamiliar territory, but there was no question about their past. "I'm not sorry I slept with you."

"Good. I hope to make it a regular occurrence for the next few weeks or so."

Her heart did a perfect backflip in her chest. Okay, that answered the one-night stand question. And, as crazy as this relationship was, as crazy as it was making her feel, she wasn't ready to give it up. But she'd worked too hard to build her business to let it slide. She'd just have to figure out how to manage extra time for Paulo. And that meant setting some ground rules.

"I want to make one thing clear," she said, tucking her hair behind her ear. "My work comes first. Everything else, including us, comes second. No exceptions."

He lifted a cynical brow. "I appreciate your dedication, especially since it benefits me as well. But I can't say I look forward to constantly competing with your never ending to-do list."

"My business is my only priority, Paulo."

"I'll accept the condition as long *you* understand one thing."

"What's that?"

A glint of mischief appeared in his eyes. "I'm going to focus all my free time on changing your mind," he said as he reached up to rub her bottom lip.

Her body basked in the electric sensation he created. She lifted her chin, fighting for what she hoped was an artless smile. "I hope you're not afraid of hard work."

Humor lit his gaze. "And you said the challenge was over."

"A girl should always keep a man guessing."

A grin crooked the side of his mouth. "With you, I never know what to expect next. Now," he said, taking her elbow, "let's go show these people what you're made of."

Looking down the hall at the lobby, she took a deep breath and squared her shoulders. She was as ready as she'd ever be. Certainly better than she'd been a few minutes ago. And it was time to clear this final hurdle. Ignoring the tension in her body, she let Paulo lead her down the hallway and into the crowd.

CHAPTER SIX

PAULO leaned back in the leather chair in his office. Twenty-four hours after the grand opening and he was still wondering what the hell had just happened. Finding his sassy event planner cowering in the staff hallway had been a surprise. For a brief moment he'd considered leaving her alone. Marriage had taught him he was no good with overly emotional women. He didn't do wedding rings anymore, and he most definitely didn't do drama.

But the look on Alyssa's face—the *panic*—had cut him in ways he hadn't imagined.

So he'd distracted her the only way he knew how. And the kiss had proved a success, and highly stimulating.

Now he was the one in need of a distraction, because he couldn't set aside the disturbing knowledge that she'd spent her teen years working. He'd assumed her childhood must have been rough, but something in the way she'd said "we needed the money" told him she was downplaying the ugly truth. And coming face to face with her hardship rankled.

An unwelcome tug snagged him somewhere deep.

Alyssa never asked for sympathy. Or pity. And if he hadn't known her so well she would have looked every bit the polite businesswoman as they'd made their way around the lobby. But her nervous habits had grown familiar: a tuck of silky hair behind her ear, the swipe of a palm down her pantsuit, the tight smile and the thicker accent.

The Reader Service - Here's how it works:

Accepting your 2 free books and 2 free mystery gifts (gifts valued at approximately $10.00) places you under no obligation to buy anything. You may keep the books and gifts and return the shipping statement marked "cancel." If you do not cancel, about a month later we'll send you 6 additional books and bill you just $4.30 each for the regular-print edition or $4.80 each for the larger-print edition in the U.S. or $4.99 each for the regular-print edition or $5.49 each for the larger-print edition in Canada. That's a savings of at least 13% off the cover price. It's quite a bargain! Shipping and handling is just 50¢ per book in the U.S. and 75¢ per book in Canada.* You may cancel at any time, but if you choose to continue, every month we'll send you 6 more books, which you may either purchase at the discount price or return to us and cancel your subscription.

*Terms and prices subject to change without notice. Prices do not include applicable taxes. Sales tax applicable in N.Y. Canadian residents will be charged applicable taxes. Offer not valid in Quebec. All orders subject to credit approval. Books received may not be as shown. Credit or debit balances in a customer's account(s) may be offset by any other outstanding balance owed by or to the customer. Please allow 4 to 6 weeks for delivery. Offer available while quantities last.

▼ If offer card is missing write to: The Reader Service, P.O. Box 1867, Buffalo, NY 14240-1867 or visit www.ReaderService.com ▼

BUSINESS REPLY MAIL

FIRST-CLASS MAIL PERMIT NO. 717 BUFFALO, NY

POSTAGE WILL BE PAID BY ADDRESSEE

THE READER SERVICE
PO BOX 1867
BUFFALO NY 14240-9952

NO POSTAGE NECESSARY IF MAILED IN THE UNITED STATES

So what had happened to his spunky event manager? Where had her gumption gone? She didn't seem the type to let mistreatment by a bunch of hypocrites bother her.

His eyebrows pulled together in deliberation.

She worked hard to maintain the stoic mask. The cool professional fixated on her work. But over time, with him, that mask had cracked wide open, and when he'd finally watched her shatter in the elevator mirror she had made him ache. And the single night they'd shared had changed everything. Making love to her. Listening to her cry out. His body coiled tight at the memory.

He'd never felt so satisfied. But after an incredible night together he'd woken up alone. Ditched without a goodbye. A scowl infiltrated his face.

Watching her come apart in his arms was addictive, but he had the impression if he left her alone she wouldn't complain. She would continue on, business as usual. Fixated on her job. And the thought left him intensely *un*satisfied.

So the challenge was far from over. Not until Alyssa learned to apply as much passion to her life as she did to her job.

His thoughts were interrupted by a knock at the door and the arrival of his Chief of Operations. Charles had a newspaper in his hand, and his navy suit looked stifling for the sweltering temperature outside. Sometimes Paulo really pitied the man.

"I have some news," Charles said as he adjusted his wire-frame glasses. "First, the Ocean Inn in Boca Raton was just placed on the market. It could be a profitable enterprise." He paused and shifted on his feet, looking uncomfortable and infinitely more grave than usual. "And your brother called today, requesting your cell phone number."

The flare of anger was instantaneous. What could Marcos possibly have to say? *I'm really enjoying your wife? Thanks for warming her up for me?*

Paulo's frown grew deeper. "I hope you told him no."

"Naturally."

"Good man, Charles."

"He left a message for you to call." There was a minor pause before Charles continued. "And one more thing before I go. I wanted to show you this. The phone has been ringing nonstop since this morning." He held out the newspaper.

At the sight, Paulo tensed, preparing for bad news. To this day he still couldn't read a headline without flinching. The mention of his brother made his response that much worse. But when one of his manager's rarely dispensed smiles appeared, Paulo relaxed.

Charles said, "It appears we're the new popular South Beach venue for an event."

Paulo reached for the society section of the local newspaper. There was a spectacular array of photos of the Samba on the front page. Wedding guests at the lobby bar. A happy bride and groom dancing. And a stunning night time picture of the roof-top decked out in all its glory. He scanned the article quickly, a grin of satisfaction crossing his face at the glowing report. "I'll have to thank our strategic partner for her outstanding work."

"Yes, sir," Charles said. "But before you do you should know that you already sent Ms. Hunt flowers, thanking her for her efforts on behalf of the Samba."

Surprised at the news, Paulo set the paper down. "How thoughtful of me," he said dryly. "What kind of flowers did I choose?"

"A delicate blend of orchids and gardenias." Charles frowned, suddenly looking concerned. "I hope you don't mind my doing so, sir."

"No, not at all, Charles. It's your job to make me look good. And you do it well."

"Thank you," he said, his somber air returning. "Have a good evening."

As Charles left, Paulo raked the hair from his forehead.

Man...he'd spent an incredible night with a stunning, sexy woman and it was his manager who had thought to send her flowers. Not for the sex, of course, but because of the bang-up job she'd done promoting his hotel. So he'd had two good reasons to send Alyssa flowers and he hadn't. Paulo frowned.

If he wasn't careful he'd wind up as self-absorbed as his brother.

With a sigh, he looked at his watch. He was supposed to meet Nick at the racetrack in two hours. His frown faded to a grin. But first there was a luscious lady down the hall he needed to see.

The sweet smell of gardenias filled her office, bringing a smile to Alyssa's face as she ticked off her day's accomplishments, happy with her progress. She'd updated her priority list, compiled the catering bids for the Mayor's birthday party, and reviewed her notes on the new audiovisual company.

Transfer of her revised to-do list complete, she disconnected her phone from her laptop just as a knock sounded in the room. Paulo poked his head through the door, a devilish look on his handsome face. And faster than a high-speed internet connection she wanted him again. Her nipples tightened in response. *Whoa.* What had this man turned her into?

"You busy?" Paulo asked.

Alyssa crossed her arms across her breasts to hide the reaction. "Depends on what you have in mind."

Paulo stepped inside, closed the door, and leaned against the wall, hands behind his back. The look he gave her made her skin tingle. "Oh, I definitely think you're going to like what I have in mind." He tipped his head, his eyes lit with mischief. "Are you done with work for the evening?"

She couldn't control her body's response to the words. Anticipation hummed, the heated blood in her veins warming her to her toes. Since their night together not ten minutes had passed without a picture of Paulo popping into her head. And in every one of them he was naked.

She really was a degenerate.

"Paulo," Alyssa said, growing serious as she glanced at the door, "I'm not sure the office is a good idea."

"Why not?" His voice took on a hint of danger, leaving no doubt what he had in mind. "It's six o'clock. Everyone in this hall is gone." Hands still behind his back, he approached her. "I locked the door." His eyes dropped to her chest and his voice turned to a throaty rumble. "And the walls are thick enough to block all that noise you'll make."

Alyssa ignored the blazing heat that flared higher. "And you won't be making any noise?"

His eyes went dark. "It turns me on just listening to you…" His voice died away, leaving Alyssa breathless, too. "Get ready to make some noise, Ms. Hunt." Paulo sent her a cocky grin and pulled his hands from behind his back, dropping a newspaper on her desk. "A little light reading for your evening enjoyment."

Confused, Alyssa reached for the paper. Across the front page was a gorgeous spread of photos of the hotel. Recovery from the abrupt turn of events was slow, but she finally managed to skim through the article, her smile growing as she registered the praise. When she reached the end she read it again, just for fun. Feeling positively giddy, she looked up at Paulo and let out a laugh.

Eyes sparkling with humor, Paulo perched on the edge of her desk. "Charles says people are clamoring to schedule the hotel for their receptions. Things are about to get even busier around here." His voice wicked with amusement, he went on, "And you thought I came in here for something else."

Alyssa shot him a scolding look, but it was half-hearted at best. "That's what you wanted me to think." Even worse, she was disappointed he'd only been teasing. She had an overwhelming urge to make him squirm in return. Her eyes landed on the gardenias. "Paulo, I meant to thank you…" She didn't have to work hard for the dreamy quality in her voice. "Sending me these beautiful flowers." She watched his grin fade, holding back her smile. "I can't tell you how much they mean to me."

For a brief moment Paulo looked positively speechless. Alyssa reached for her phone, snapping a photo of him.

"What was the picture for?" He asked, clearly stumped by the sequence of events.

Alyssa let out a small laugh. "To capture the struggle on your face as you worked out how to explain the flowers weren't from you."

"How did you know?"

Alyssa pulled the card from the arrangement, releasing the scent of gardenias, and read, *"'Dear Ms. Hunt. Thank you so much for your efforts. Your diligence, efficiency and attention to detail made for a delightful evening. Sincerely, Mr. Domingues.'"*

Alyssa arched an eyebrow. "Either Charles sent it…" she lobbed him a look as she tossed the card on her desk "…or you need to work on your moves, Mr. Domingues."

"There's nothing wrong with my moves." He grinned down at her, and his voice dropped. "You want me to show you one of them now?"

Stunned, she bit the tip of her tongue. Yes. She wanted to tell him *yes*! It was what a modern woman would do. Take charge of her sexuality. Embrace the temptation that was consuming her. Her temperature spiraled higher, and she opened her mouth to answer.

But a randy rendezvous on her desk would be way out of line.

At the last second she chickened out, glancing at the cell phone in her hand. "I still need an hour or so to answer my messages."

The moment the wimpy words left her lips she wanted them

back. A look of challenge flashed in Paulo's eyes, as if she'd thrown down a gauntlet. And then his gaze turned from milk chocolate to dark.

He took her phone, set it aside, and lifted her chin with his finger. "Maybe I should remind you of what you're missing."

Heat infused her limbs, leaving them weightless, and she waited in anticipation as Paulo leaned forward and touched his mouth to hers. Small whisper-kisses. Subtle, feathery kisses. A gentle exploration that was more of a tease than a touch—until he finally opened her mouth with his. Her lips went soft, and her body followed close behind. With a sigh, she leaned into him.

She'd missed this. It had only been three days, but she missed how he made her feel. The delicious slide of tongue on tongue left her craving more.

And more was what she got when Paulo hoisted her onto the edge of the desk. With his mouth still on hers, he pushed her skirt high, and she wiggled her hips to aid his efforts. She didn't mount a peep of a protest when his hands slid under her blouse to release the front clasp of her bra. He cupped her bare breasts, and his thumbs began to circle her nipples. The tips tingled, grew hard, and her groan was loud against his lips.

He leaned back to watch her face, his breathing heavy. As his hands drove her temperature to critical, he whispered, "Shall I go and come back in an hour?"

Eyelids stretched wide, she stared at him. Not fair. He was teasing her. And how did he manage to get her so hot and bothered while he still had the power to pull back? She frowned. "Listen, mister," she said with a decided twang. She grabbed his shirt and hauled him closer, pulling him firmly between her legs. "Don't you *dare*."

The brash demand and bawdy action brought a warm flush to her cheeks. Maybe she'd been too aggressive? One night together and she thought she'd learned all she needed to know.

Had experienced everything. It was frightening to discover she hadn't plumbed the full extent of her passion, her sexuality. Just how deep did it go?

And how lewd could she get?

But the grin on Paulo's face was huge. "That was hot."

And then he kissed her again, hard, as if inspired, chasing away the doubts. His tongue stroked hers in time with the drag of his thumbs across her nipples. Swallowing her moans, Paulo thrust his hips, his hardness rubbing against her center until Alyssa was so ready for him she let out a cry and dug her nails into the tight muscles of his backside. A wordless plea to end her agony. To be filled. By Paulo. No other man would do. Her response to him was singularly unique. Special.

Paulo pulled back again, his eyes dark with desire. "I don't have a condom."

Shocked by the cruel news, she choked back a sob of protest.

Hands on her breasts, his tone was firm, insistent. "What else do you want?"

Her blood turned to sludge in her veins, her heart so loud in her ears it was hard to hear. "I don't know."

"Yes, you do." The frank honesty in his face didn't budge. "So say it."

Seconds ticked by. "I can't." Oh, dear God, why did she always sound so juvenile? At twenty-eight, too. How lame was that?

His hands dropped to her hips, his gaze refusing to give. "Try anyway."

She opened her mouth, but couldn't speak. Every time she thought of a response memories choked it, the long-ago words whispering in her head: Trashy. Easy. *Slut.*

But she wanted him so much. And as she stared at his dazzling face the alluring promise in his eyes sent a frisson of excitement up her spine. She was torn with this desire that effortlessly destroyed her cool faster than the old fear could rebuild it. Until she couldn't take it anymore.

Alyssa slowly leaned back on the desk, lifted her hips, and slid her panties down. If the words were too hard, she would show him. She tossed her underwear aside and spread her legs, begging him with her eyes.

His gaze burned into hers, and he laid a scorching hand on her bare thigh. "That's a good start." He didn't move, and the waiting expectation on his face slayed her all over again.

"Just a start?" she said.

"I want you to trust me enough to tell me what you want."

Her chest clenched tighter around her heart. "I'm happy with whatever you give."

"No." His hand gripped her thigh and he leaned forward, looking down at her with an intensity that was compelling. "That's not enough."

Tears of frustration stung her lids. He demanded too much. The impossible.

"I'm afraid I'll sound vulgar," she whispered, closing her eyes, terrified at the thought. "Or crude."

He laid a hand on her cheek and she lifted her lids. "Alyssa." His voice was soft, his gaze tender. "You couldn't sound crude if you tried."

And then Paulo shifted down her body, casting gentle kisses on her skin as he went, murmuring reassurances. When he got to her inner thigh, her legs trembled. Anticipation surged as his lips drew close to where she wanted them, where she *needed* them to kiss her. But he hovered at the edge, not giving her what she wanted. Her body burned. Ached.

She was one giant nerve-ending, waiting on Paulo.

He opened her with his fingers, his words whispering across her swollen, sensitized skin. "Say it, Alyssa," he demanded.

"Please." Her voice broke. "Take me in your mouth."

His lips closed around her nub and suckled. The wicked

touch seared her nerves and Alyssa let out a cry, arching her back. Cradling her buttocks, he brought her closer, and she almost wept with relief.

She was lost in a sea of sensation. Riding high and growing ever higher. Waves of pleasure swelled, and then receded. Each time cresting to new heights, sweeping her along in a treacherous current until she was too raw with need, too exposed to care anymore.

Breathless, she threaded her fingers through his hair and told him what she wanted. More pressure. Or less. Faster, or slower.

The pleasure was eating her alive. Spreading her legs wider, she strained up toward the unrelenting sensation. And her words grew bold, explicit. Until she was demanding the rake of his teeth, or the slick slide of his tongue.

And he obliged. Feeding her fantasy.

Until a final rasp of his tongue drew a loud groan from her lips, sparks bursting behind her lids. She clutched his head, the orgasm washing through her with shimmering waves of fire and light…and the delicious feel of her sex clenching beneath his mouth.

Forty-five minutes later Paulo steered the Ducati into the circular drive at the Samba. Tense didn't begin to describe how he felt. The word failed to capture the tumultuous battle for supremacy raging in his body.

And just who was in control here? Him or his hormones?

After their tryst in her office—and the hint of a sexually assertive side to Alyssa—he'd muttered a weak excuse and bolted to take a cold shower in one of the hotel rooms, hoping to extinguish the blazing fire. Massive fail. Thinking a ride would help, he'd gone for a spin around the block.

Unfortunately, getting caught doing a hundred in a thirty-mile-an-hour zone wasn't an option, and the painfully slow putter behind a pack of sightseers had only exacerbated the agony.

What he needed was a full-throttle, high-speed race around the track. Because not a tiny dent was made in his need for her.

With a frown, he parked his bike by the front curb of the Samba. What was wrong with him? He'd never had this kind of trouble with a woman before. Letting an affair run roughshod through his life. Clearly, with the emergence of the racier Alyssa, he'd have to try a little harder.

As a stretch BMW pulled up behind him, Paulo dismounted the Ducati. He stepped on the kickstand, ignoring the limo until a familiar figure emerged from inside. The sight shot his mood from agitated to outright antagonistic. His body went rigid. Stunned, he flipped up the visor on his helmet and watched his brother approach. In an Italian suit and leather shoes worn with the intent to impress, he strode toward Paulo like he owned the Samba. Which he didn't.

Not anymore.

Marcos stopped a few feet away. He'd aged since their last apocalyptic meeting; his short dark hair now had a hint of gray at the temples. The hard face and set of his mouth were just like their dad's, all the way down to the disapproval in his eyes. But Paulo had never cared what Marcos thought of him, only his father.

The sheer nerve of his brother to show up at this hotel had Paulo seething, teeth grating as he pulled off his helmet. Reining in the familiar fury, he turned his back on Marcos and hung his helmet on a handle. "What are you doing here?"

"If you had returned my message, you would know."

The curt response drove Paulo's anger higher, but he'd be drawn and quartered before he'd let Marcos see how much his presence affected him. "I have nothing to say to you." He headed for the entrance to the hotel. Nearing the doorman, he jerked a thumb in the direction of his motorcycle. "Keep an eye on her, will you, Jerry?"

The elderly man tipped his uniformed cap. "Sure thing, Mr. Domingues."

Paulo was a few feet up the granite staircase when Marcos's voice called out.

"Believe it or not, Paulo, this isn't all about you. This is about Dad's will."

The sharp, indignant stab of resentment brought Paulo to a halt. "Dad's will?" He turned to look down on his brother, annoyed to see he was following him. "That was years ago. He gave you the company. And, sorry, I sold the shares of Domingues International he left me to buy my first hotel." He shot Marcos a piercing look. "You can't have those, too."

Apparently being sole heir had left Marcos feeling a touch guilty—or maybe it was the fact he'd pilfered Paulo's wife—because his eye twitched at one corner. "Quit being so difficult."

The irony sent Paulo's eyebrows skyward. "*I'm* being difficult?" He knew from a lifetime of experience that, if he didn't get Marcos to leave they would end up goading one another until it disintegrated into an ugly debate. Paulo sent him an empty smile. "If you don't like my attitude, feel free to go, big brother."

Paulo pivoted on his heel and nodded as Jerry held open the front door. He crossed the busy lobby and moved down the hallway leading to his office, managing to resist the urge to slam the door behind him as he headed for his desk. The forest-green walls of his office were soothing. But, even better, they didn't contain his brother.

The sound of the door opening behind him made his insides twist. Damn, the man wasn't going away. Hoping to keep his hands busy—and maybe control his anger—Paulo picked up his autographed baseball as he rounded his desk. He flopped into his leather chair and leaned back, propping his feet next to his computer and waiting for Marcos to speak.

Frowning, his brother strode into the room. “Don’t walk away from me.”

The arrogance was familiar, but no less infuriating. “My hotel. My rules.” Paulo began tossing the ball lightly in his hand. “I’ll do whatever I want.”

“I see you still dress like a slob.”

“You got something against jeans and a motocross T-shirt?”

Marcos pushed his Armani jacket back, hands on his hips, gold Rolex gleaming in the light. “Never mind your appalling lack of couth, we need to discuss Dad’s will.”

The old resentment flared again, and he was getting tired of its return. Paulo gripped the baseball tight, fighting the need to hurl it at the wall. “There’s nothing to discuss.”

“Dad left me with a job that I intend to complete. I was put in charge of a trust that comes into effect on the fifth anniversary of his death,” Marcos said, his mouth white, pinched with anger. “Did you even realize how long it’s been?”

“Yeah,” Paulo replied slowly. “I’m well aware of the date.” Even though it was hard to miss a father who barely noticed you were alive, his passing had still hit Paulo hard. Because it had been the end of any hope for a little praise from the man.

And those dark days had been about more than just the loss of his dad.

“Which means yours and Bianca’s wedding anniversary is coming up, too.” Paulo hiked a scornful brow. “Shall I send you two a card? I could draw little red hearts on the envelope if you like.”

Marcos ignored the remarks and plowed on, lines of aggravation engraved around his mouth. “You were named a beneficiary of Dad’s trust. It leaves you an additional fifty-million-dollar inheritance.”

Paulo tossed the ball onto his desk. It landed with a thunk and rolled off to hit the floor.

Money. Always about the damn money. It was the only kind

of success his dad had understood. And after investing years of hard work, with barely a word of acknowledgment from his old man, the final insult had come at his father's death. Marcos's role as the favorite child had payed off big-time when he was handed the throne.

And now Paulo had been beaten out by his brother for his dad's attention one final time.

His gut buckled under the weight of the memory. "I'm not interested."

"Don't be childish."

Paulo couldn't believe the words. After the stunt Marcos had pulled, he was calling *him* childish?

"Dad wanted you to have it," his brother went on.

"Your wife is addicted to the finer things in life. She couldn't stand the thought she might have to live on less." Paulo speared his fingers through his hair. "So why don't you give the money to her?"

Marcos didn't move, and something unrecognizable flickered in his eyes. "Money isn't the reason Bianca left you."

The verbal smack hit Paulo hard, and his hand landed on the desk with a thump. "She left me when I threatened to leave the company, hooked up with you, and then took another vow of forever right after you inherited it all." He cocked his head in disbelief. "That's a helluva coincidence."

Marcos's titanium steel gaze bored into Paulo's. "You never did understand her."

Undaunted, Paulo stood up from his chair, staring back. "I understand her better than you think." He would not waste his time debating his ex-wife with his brother. "It's time for you to go."

Face red, Marcos looked ready to blow. "We'll discuss this again later."

Paulo nodded toward the door. "This discussion is over."

CHAPTER SEVEN

ALYSSA sat in the empty bleachers, bathed in the light of the setting sun. The rumbling roar grew louder as the pack of motorcycles zoomed by, leaving the acrid smell of hot rubber in its wake. Alyssa held her breath as Paulo leaned deep to take the curve, his knee almost dragging the pavement. When he was safely around Alyssa relaxed, remembering to inhale.

Everything about the man left her breathless. And when Paulo had stopped back at her office to invite her along for his practice run she should have said no. But she'd said yes. Partly because she was still dazed from the moment on her desk an hour earlier. And partly because…well, because she wanted to.

It had been so easy for Paulo to sidetrack her today. What started as a simple kiss had turned her into someone she hadn't recognized. And she still couldn't believe some of the things she'd said to him.

Worrying the button on her cuff, she watched Paulo pull off to the side and dismount, the first one to finish. His lean form was encased in a protective racing suit. The uniform only increased the man's sex appeal, and her body started that crazy internal cha-cha again. She let out a self-directed, chastising snort.

Paulo Domingues, able to take a woman from borderline frigid to knocking on nympho in ten seconds flat.

When Paulo headed into the concession stand, her tension

eased a touch. And then the second place finisher parked next to Paulo's Ducati, flipped up the visor on his helmet, and scanned the bleachers. Surprised, Alyssa watched him lope up the stairs in her direction.

"You must be Alyssa." He came to a stop in front of her bench, propping a foot on the seat beside her. "Nick Tatum," he said as he pulled off his headgear. "Owner of the hottest nightclub in South Beach and Paulo's oldest friend." He stuck out a hand, his green eyes twinkling. "In duration, that is, not in age."

Alyssa returned the shake, laughing at his disclaimer. "Nice to meet you."

He was good looking in an all-American way, his brown hair sun kissed with glints of gold. "Anything you want to know about Paulo, just ask."

Alyssa studied him closely. A very noteworthy statement. And one that left her wondering if it was a warning. But she kept her tone light. "Is there anything in particular you think I should know?"

A rakish grin appeared. "A very perceptive woman, I see." He paused before going on. "But on second thought…" He tipped his head. "I wouldn't want to kill the mystery."

"Is mystery a good thing or a bad thing?"

He leaned closer, as if sharing a secret, his grin so big Alyssa had to smile. "Depends on who you ask," he said.

Paulo appeared behind his friend, a tray laden with two hot dogs in his hand. "Are you done flirting?" The tone was easy.

Too easy. Because Paulo's expression was hard, his eyes sharp. The moment froze, tension snapping in the air like heat lightning on a summer evening.

Nick's forehead furrowed in amusement. "Ease up, bro." Removing his foot from beside Alyssa, he straightened up. "I'm not moving in on your territory."

Paulo switched his gaze to Alyssa. "I didn't say you were."

He held a hot dog in her direction and took a seat in the exact spot where Nick's foot had been.

The position was intentional, and Alyssa bit back the laugh, strangely tickled at Paulo's discomfort. It was such an unexpected turn of events. But she should at least pretend to be offended. As she reached for the hot dog, she shot them both a grow-up look. "Territory?" she said dryly. "Is that really a term you two use?"

"Hell, no," Paulo said.

"At least not in mixed company," Nick added. "My Neanderthal-looking friend here is exuding more testosterone than usual, so it seemed appropriate." Paulo was now scowling outright, but a grin lit Nick's face. "But don't worry," he said as he clapped Paulo's shoulder. "I just wanted to meet Alyssa and find out what's responsible for your win tonight." The man rubbed his chin with a finger. "Whatever it is that has you bugged, you sure seemed willing to put your life in peril."

As he looked at Alyssa, Nick jerked his head in Paulo's direction and continued. "Watching him bang his head against the wall in frustration might be more fun than Lady Gaga in concert, but it's also a guarantee he'll risk life and limb to beat me on the track."

Alyssa looked curiously at Paulo.

But by now Paulo's face was bland, and he lifted a brow at his friend. "Are you going to stand there and be helpful all night?"

"Easy on the sarcasm, my friend. You might hurt yourself." Nick shot Paulo another grin, obviously undaunted by his friend's hint to leave. "I'm just keepin' it real." He looked down at the hot dog Alyssa was holding. "By the way, in case you didn't know, Paulo's loaded." Eyes sparkling, he nodded at her food. "You should hold out for a better dinner. And now," Nick said, sending his friend a salute, "she's all yours." He shot Alyssa a wink and then turned to lope back down the bleachers.

Nick's comments were interesting, because she had sensed

Paulo's strained, almost dark mood when he'd picked her up. Gazing out over the track, she ate her hot dog, pondering the source.

Finally, she had to ask. "Why do you take the risk?" When he sent her a questioning look, she nodded toward the track. "The dangerous speeds. The death-defying corners." She shook her head. "It's crazy."

He gave a careless shrug. "The key to speed is keeping tight control over your bike."

Remembering their blistering encounters, her voice went low. "You like to keep everything under your control, don't you?"

Paulo lifted a brow, his eyes now glowing with amusement. "Let's not turn this into an attempt to psychoanalyze my personality." He looked at her half-eaten hot dog and then at her, his voice rumbling sensually. "Now, finish up so I can take you home."

The promise in his statement had her heart rate doing double time, creating a hum of desire as she stared at him, her insides twirling. Clever little maneuver he had there, wielding his charm to redirect the conversation.

After finishing her hot dog, she leaned back on her hands and watched him polish off his food. "It's not going to work, you know." His eyebrows lifted in question, and she tipped her head. "Trying to seduce me with the adrenaline-junkie attitude."

"It won't?"

"I'm afraid not."

"Hmm." His voice low, he leaned in, bringing those better-than-chocolate eyes closer. "What will it take?"

Desire skipped along her nerves. Shoot. She really needed to work on being harder to get. "Sorry," she said softly. "But I have to make you suffer a little first."

His gaze moved to her mouth. "As if you hadn't already," Paulo said. "The Alyssa that finally came out to play today was inspiring." His voice dropped to a rough whisper. "I've never been so turned on in my life."

She bit her lip, her heart thumping. "I was a bit…graphic."

"Oh, yeah. And I want more from where that came from," he growled. He narrowed his eyes. "But maybe you should wait until I have the equipment to follow through."

"Consider it revenge for shamelessly seducing a woman who was trying to work."

His lips twitched. "I look forward to letting you seduce me instead." He stood and took Alyssa's hand, pulling her to her feet. "We can start the celebration of my win with a drink at your place," he said, and turned to lead her down the steps.

The words and his tone, combined with the feel of her fingers entwined with his, sent her desire heavenward. Suddenly, exerting a bit of control of her own seemed vital. "Are you inviting yourself over to my apartment?" she scolded, her tone teasing. She gently shook her head. "Your invitation. Your idea." They reached the ground and headed in the direction of the Ducati. She sent him a deliberate look. "I think it should be at your place."

Every fiber in Paulo's being immediately balked at the idea, and he fought the need to frown. Listening to the gravel crunch beneath their feet, he was careful to keep his expression shuttered as he wrestled with the thought of her at his house.

Because it went against his rules. He kept his affairs separate from his private life. Out of his home. Out of his space. It made it easier to get them out of his life. And the thought of *Alyssa* in his bed was like moving too fast into a curve, flirting with disaster. Knowing one false move and their relationship would spin out from under him, hurtling them both toward a painful crash.

He didn't want to give her the wrong impression. And he sure as hell didn't want to think about all the reasons this woman was a risk to his hard-earned peace of mind. All he wanted was to get lost in the rare chemistry they shared. To watch Alyssa enjoy it, too. Especially after the day he'd had…

Wound tight from his seduction efforts. Enduring his brother's visit. And now his ridiculous reaction when he saw his friend standing so close to Alyssa.

And why had seeing them together bugged him so much? Nick was an accomplished flirt. He hit on every female he found easy on the eye. But just because Nick managed to make Alyssa laugh, it didn't mean anything. And even if it *did* mean something, it shouldn't bother him. The jealousy was new, sophomoric, and damn irrational.

All the more reason to stick to the *Paulo's Plans for Dating Handbook*.

"It would be easier if we went to your apartment," he said.

She stopped, forcing him to halt beside her. "Who said anything about making this easy?" With a light tone, she continued. "Those are my terms. Take it or leave it."

Clutching her hand, Paulo looked out over the mostly vacant parking lot. Every time he tried to teach Alyssa a lesson, he was the one who paid the price. He blew out a frustrated breath and took in her exquisite face, leaning in close. "Like I have a choice."

Her eyes sparkled with humor. "You always have a choice, Mr. Domingues."

Paulo stared at her, enjoying her look of amusement. Her sweet scent grew stronger as he swept the hair from her cheek. Her gaze turned dark at his touch, and his body grew tight. "No," he murmured. "I don't think I do."

After providing a tour of the Samba facilities, Alyssa said goodbye to the couple searching for a reception site and took a seat at the rooftop bar to jot down her notes. The bartender set an iced tea in front of her, and Alyssa nodded her thanks.

The Atlantic sparkled in the distance. Soaking up the warm

midday rays, guests relaxed in lounge chairs or took a dip in the cool water of the pool.

Normally she would consider the relaxing view a distraction. But her desk, where memories of Paulo were vivid, was worse. And, after the fabulously successful wedding reception, work was getting busy. Every day her to-do list grew longer. But she was having trouble focusing, thanks to her disturbingly handsome, insanely seductive client.

Last evening, after leaving the track, Paulo had taken her to his house and straight to his bed. Another jaw-dropping, amazing night. Sometimes she'd led and sometimes she'd followed, but she had never hesitated to tell him what she wanted. And the sense of empowerment had been liberating. Paulo had enjoyed it, too.

She'd thought she'd won a victory when he agreed to take her to his home. But when she'd opened her eyes at dawn, a gentle light had lit the bedroom walls filled with racing photographs, baseball memorabilia, and pictures of historic hotels in South Beach. A smile had crept up her face when she'd spied a pair of jeans draped over a chair. It was all so much more personal than a cold, sterile hotel room.

But he hadn't wanted to bring her there, insisting from the beginning this was a short-term affair. And her smile had died as she was struck by the thought that, suddenly, she wasn't satisfied.

Their temporary arrangement had allowed her to ignore her doubts and indulge in a little free time with a funny, sexy, drop-dead gorgeous man who made her feel things she hadn't thought possible. A temporary arrangement which had seemed perfect… until now.

Unnerved, she had crept downstairs, called a taxi, and gone home. After a quick shower and change of clothes she'd arrived at the office early, desperately burying her worries in the familiar routine of work.

Ice shifted in her glass with a clink, and she realized most of it had melted. Frowning, she glanced at her watch. She'd been sitting there for fifteen minutes. Doing nothing.

Okay, girl. You have *so* got to get your head together.

Pen poised in her hand, she stared at her blank notepad. But every five minutes her mind drifted back to the fact that she was now unhappy with the limits on their relationship. Apprehension whittled away a little more of her courage, and she set her pen aside, giving up on the task.

She picked up her cold glass and pressed it to her cheek, heart tapping loudly. Her mind churned with questions. How was she going to handle this growing desire to have more of him in her life? And would he even be interested in an ex-con as a steady girlfriend?

"I woke up alone again."

Alyssa jerked and set down her glass, turning in her seat. Paulo was in a T-shirt and cut-offs, every muscle in his arms and legs exposed. Her mouth went as dry as hot sand baking on a beach.

Heart hammering harder, she carefully controlled her expression. "I have a lot I want to accomplish today," she said evenly.

He leaned against the counter, bringing a deluge of images from their night together. She wrapped her hand around her chilled glass, fighting the warmth he generated, vainly trying to steady her heart. Obviously overexposure to Paulo's touch was *not* desensitizing her to his presence.

"You could give a guy a complex," Paulo said dryly.

Alyssa bit the inside of her cheek, repressing the threat of a nervous giggle. The thought of Paulo with confidence issues was laughable. "Just trying to please my new client," she said.

His eyes lingered on her face. "You already have," he murmured.

"Then why the complaint?"

"Did you enjoy last night?" he asked.

"You know I did."

"So why is your work so important you'd choose to spend a Saturday morning here rather than in my bed?"

As he scrutinized her face, he seemed to be waiting for her to respond. But her budding doubts about their relationship and his disturbing proximity momentarily left her speechless. And then a glimmer of determination finally appeared in his eyes.

"I was hoping to convince you to share the reason by upgrading my dinner plans from the racetrack to the top of the Ritz." He paused and cocked his head inquisitively, as if waiting for an answer. "Best restaurant in town… Excellent mojitos…"

A jumble of confused feelings ensued. Their discussion at the grand opening had probably left him believing she was a downtrodden former juvenile delinquent who'd never been given a fair shot. But what would he think if she told him the whole story? The reason why her work was so important?

Blowing out a breath, she eyed him warily. "You're asking me out on a date?"

Humor lit Paulo's face. "I'm asking you out on a date."

Nibbling on a nail, she considered the offer. Essentially, she had two choices. End this affair, or push it forward. At least dinner at a nice restaurant would signal a step toward a more conventional relationship. And if it just so happened she worked up the nerve for a full disclosure—a swell of nausea tumbled in her stomach—well, at least the public location would keep his response tolerable. She let out a small sigh. "Okay."

"Good. I already had one of the staff make dinner reservations for eight," Paulo said. "I'll pick you up at seven-thirty." His expression was one of a man with a target in sight.

And Alyssa could almost see the bright bull's-eye glowing on her past.

The limousine was an unexpected surprise, but not Paulo's lack of a coat and tie. His dark pants and navy dress shirt were nice complementing Alyssa's royal blue blouse and skirt. As they exited the elevator onto the top floor of the posh high-rise, the snobby hostess started to protest Paulo's lack of proper attire. But when they stepped closer, recognition abruptly changed the woman's attitude.

So did the smile Paulo flashed her.

Alyssa watched the exchange with awe. Paulo lived in a world where people were happy to give him what he wanted. Where a respected name and oodles of money opened doors closed to others. The complete inverse of her world.

Her history slammed doors firmly in her face. Did she have the nerve to share the complete unvarnished truth?

Tension filled her body as the hostess led them to a table with a spectacular view of skyscrapers, the lights of Miami blazing against the night sky. Nestled in the corner, their secluded location detracted from the safety of a restaurant full of people. Paulo held out her chair, his fingers brushing her shoulder as he took her seat.

The scorching feel of Paulo's skin stung her nerves, and her concentration faltered. After lacing her fingers in her lap, he drew in a breath to psych herself up while he sat down and placed their drink order.

When the hostess left, Paulo settled back. One corner of his lips lifted. "I recognize that expression on your face."

Unless he'd seen her being led before a firing squad, she was pretty sure he didn't.

She'd spent a long time preparing for—and dreading—this conversation. Wondering how honest she should be. But they ould sit here until kingdom come, and she still wouldn't be eady.

And then his half-smile turned into a full one, tripping up er focus. Dark hair framed the square-cut features and slash f eyebrows. But, as usual, it was the speckled milk-chocolate eyes that held her attention. Or maybe it was the sexy curve of his mouth?

"You have that determined look on your face again." He crossed his arms, and his shirt stretched across broad shoulders, blitzing her last coherent thought. "All I want from you is the truth."

The truth. Well, there was a mood killer. And he had no idea what he was asking.

She dropped her gaze to the table, her voice soft. "Sometimes it's uglier than you think."

"It can't be that bad."

The outright confidence in his voice brought her gaze back to his. "That just proves how much you don't know."

"I'm a big boy." He looked so relaxed. So at ease with his request. Totally clueless as to what he was letting himself in for. "I'm sure I can deal with whatever you have to tell me."

"Can you?" She laid her hands flat on the table and leaned forward, looking at Paulo with total concentration. "What if the reality of my life is more truth than you can handle?"

"Alyssa," he said dryly, a faint look of amusement on his face. "Your life isn't a remake of *A Few Good Men*. There's nothing you can tell me that I can't handle."

"I was six years old the first time I helped my mother steal a box of cereal."

The humorous glint was doused from his eyes and his body went still.

Little did he know she was just getting started. Alyssa met his gaze, realizing if she looked away her courage would falter. She supposed she could have eased into that statement, but his absolute faith in his capacity to understand had finally pushed her over the edge.

And there was nothing like jumping in with both feet. Because then there was no changing your mind.

But, boy, the cold shock to the system was more effective than five iced lattes.

As they stared at each other the waiter appeared, placing their drinks on the table. Without sparing him a glance, Paulo ordered the special for them both, and the man retreated again, leaving them alone. Alyssa held his gaze as she took a sip of her mojito. The fresh mint, lime and rum were refreshing, and the alcohol warmed her stomach, relaxing her a touch.

Which could only help—because this went beyond the professional. Beyond his belief in her ability to do her job. And when had his *personal* opinion come to mean so much?

Her stomach did a sickening slow roll, but she forged ahead. There was no backing out now. "It was ridiculously easy, you know," she said. "I snuck out with the box under my sweater while my mother distracted the clerk. And who would ever suspect a kindergartner as an accomplice?" Her lips twisted wryly. "Of course, considering it was eighty degrees outside, the sweater should have been a red flag."

After a long pause, his face stunned, he said quietly, "You were so young."

"Yes. I was."

He picked up his drink with a frown. "How often did you have to do that?"

Alyssa scrunched up her face at the impossible question. She was digging herself deeper and deeper into a gaping pit. "Whenever the money ran out before our month did. Which was frequent when I was little, but dwindled to a rarity by the time I started high school."

Paulo seemed to recover from the initial shock, and with a muttered curse he plopped his glass down. "I can't believe your *mother* taught you how."

His defense of her wasn't a surprise. But it also wasn't fair.

"My mom is…" Alyssa shifted her gaze to the window, looking beyond the lights to the black sky above "…frequently frustrating, often intentionally obtuse, and occasionally incomprehensible." She let out a little huff of surrender. The description really didn't do her mother justice. "When I was in second grade I found this pretty little notebook with a beagle on it. I loved it, and I needed one for school. But of course we had no money. So I took it." She gave an apologetic shrug at the words. Good grief, no wonder he had that expression on his face. "My mom made me take it back."

Paulo looked dumbfounded. "So stealing cereal was okay but a notebook wasn't?"

"Welcome to the world of my mother." With a sigh, Alyssa leaned back. All of his judgment seemed directed at her mom. How could she explain the unexplainable? "She had a very definite idea of what was allowed and what wasn't. Cereal or a jar of peanut butter was fine. Potato chips and soda were out. Which would lead one to assume it was based on nutritional content, except an occasional candy bar was okay—but only if it was chocolate." Knowing it didn't make sense, she sent him a weak smile. "I never could figure out her logic. Then again—" she slowly shook her head "—I often still can't."

"Faulty logic." Brows furrowed, as if struggling to comprehend, he went on. "She taught a kindergartner it was okay to steal."

"When I was born, my mother was fourteen..." Alyssa leaned forward again, scanning his eyes. "*Fourteen.* A runaway foster kid who had absolutely no trust in the social welfare system. She did what she had to do to survive."

"Refusing to accept government help wasn't fair to you."

"At first she was afraid they'd take me away. After a while, the way of life became a trap."

Paulo shook his head, his hair falling across his forehead. He pushed it back, looking unconvinced. "I appreciate your loyalty to your mother. And I also realize that I have no comparable experience to draw from, but—"

"That's right," she interjected in a low voice. "Unless you've gone to bed hungry, you don't." She refused to soften her gaze. Or reduce the strength in her tone. "Judgment is easy from a comfortable, cushy distance."

They stared at each other, and the galaxy of differences between them expanded to include a new solar system. He couldn't understand. It was too much to ask of anyone. Which was why she never had. Until now. She rubbed her forehead, trying to remember why.

"So what changed?" Paulo said.

She pushed aside the doubt. "Ironically enough, it was my arrest in high school." She propped her elbows on the table. "With the money from my catering job, suddenly we didn't have to choose between eating and paying the electric bill anymore. And that was it. My mother declared stealing was no longer allowed and—boom." She spread out her hands. "We were done. And from then on, as far as she was concerned, we have always been law-abiding citizens." And her mother had avoided all conversations on the matter since.

Even when Alyssa had slipped up again.

Damn.

With trembling fingers, she reached for her drink, the guilt eating at her. "We were both ready to put it all behind us, and my catering job was the way out."

"Was that what college was? A way out?"

The queasy feeling returned, and she abandoned her glass. "Yes. I thought after two years of clean living, good grades in high school and working hard at my job I was ready to take on Osten College." Her lips twisted wryly as she laid her cheek against her palm. "Even now, I'm still amazed at my own stupidity."

Frustration carved on his face, he leaned forward, his eyes boring into hers. A prickle of shock and awareness skittered down her spine, dispersing her thoughts. She fought to control the rate of her heart and her breathing as he spoke.

"I don't get it. You have so many choices as an event planner." His face full of doubt, he said, "Why would you choose to work with the class of society you fear?"

Jeez, what a hopelessly loaded question.

Struggling to cover the emotion, she dropped her gaze to her hand, trailing a trembling finger on the tablecloth. "I'm not afraid of them, really. I just…" Her voice died. She opened her mouth to try again, but nothing came out. She knew she needed to go on, but was unsure how to finish the story. After deliberating for hours, she still didn't know.

How could she explain she wasn't worried about being exposed to their ridicule again? The ultra-wealthy of the world only served as a reminder that her ultimate humiliation was due to her own failure. Her *weakness*.

Up until now, his skepticism had been directed at her mother. Alyssa gripped the napkin in her lap. All in defense of *her*. But what about when he learned what she'd done in college? Would he lose all respect for her? There would be no more outrage on her behalf, for sure. And any illusion he had of her innocence would be killed cold. Tears pricked the back of her lids, and she turned her face to the window.

God, was she destined to be stuck in this spiral of shame forever?

"Paulo," a feminine voice called out.

With a colossal sense of relief at the interruption, Alyssa turned to see an elegant redhead approach. In a strapless black dress, she had her arm wrapped around the elbow of a man who seemed vaguely familiar, a massive diamond ring on her finger. "I stopped by the Samba this afternoon to invite you over for dinner, but your reception clerk told me you were out." Her smile was so bright Alyssa thought she would go blind from the flash of white. "Fortunately she was kind enough to tell me about your plans to dine here with Ms. Hunt."

When Alyssa pivoted her gaze to Paulo, the look on his face put an end to her relief at the interruption. If his expression and the white-knuckled grip on his glass were any indication, this would be no pleasant interlude.

Paulo's voice was soft, but his face was hard. "What are you up to, Bianca?"

The name came from the blue and blindsided Alyssa, knocking the breath from her lungs.

Bianca. Paulo's ex-wife.

Which meant the man looked familiar because he was Paulo's brother. Though he was sporting a gorgeous black suit, and his dark hair was cropped short, he was as tall as Paulo, with a matching bitter expression to boot.

Either she didn't notice, or didn't care, but Bianca's face didn't register Paulo's terse manner as she glibly pressed on. "I thought Marcos and I could join you for a drink." The redhead turned to Alyssa. "I was hoping to get these stubborn men together to discuss the money Paulo's father left him. You don't mind if we join you for a moment, do you?"

Alyssa's mind scrambled for a diplomatic response, but Bianca didn't wait, reaching to pull out a chair.

Paulo didn't bother with diplomacy. "I mind." His words stopped the woman cold. And, though he was talking to his ex-wife, his gaze was fixed on his brother. "I will not pretend we're a happy family sharing a pre-dinner drink."

A flicker of annoyance came and went in Bianca's eyes. The tension upgraded from uncomfortable to stifling, triggering a pause that ground out the seconds into a sci-fi-worthy time warp that lasted forever. Alyssa shifted uncomfortably in her seat, her gaze moving from Bianca, to Paulo, and then to his brother.

Marcos's expression was one step away from pure stone.

"This is a waste of time, Bianca." The man said nothing to his brother. "He won't discuss the trust."

The woman turned to her husband, still oddly upbeat. "I'm sure Paulo will be reasonable."

"No, I won't." And without further explanation Paulo stood. "So, if you'll excuse us, Alyssa and I will be leaving."

Bianca's shiny veneer cracked, her desperation oozing to the surface, while Marcos's face took the final step, taking on a look of granite. But at least he was finally acknowledging his brother's presence, even if it was with a glare.

Paulo tossed a thick wad of money on the table and shot Marcos a smile laced with sarcasm. "Enjoy the meal. And give our regards to the waiter."

Desperate to escape the unhappy atmosphere, Alyssa began to stand, but stopped when Bianca touched her arm. "I believe we have an acquaintance in common, Alyssa." Her rediscovered smile would have done Malibu Barbie proud.

What a piece of work. How could she stand there and pretend everything was fine?

Bianca went on. "At the South Beach Historic Society's luncheon yesterday I ran into Tessa Harrison. We were discussing the wonderful newspaper article about the Meyer reception when your name came up."

The blood in Alyssa's face made a beeline for her toes; it was a good thing she was still sitting or she might have collapsed. No doubt Tessa Harrison had gleefully described Alyssa's arrest. And as her heart rate slowed, each beat growing more forceful than the last, she was sure the thudding vibration would shake the table.

"I have a party I'm planning at the country club." Bianca pulled a business card from her clutch purse and held it out to Alyssa. "I could use some expert advice. Perhaps you could call me sometime to discuss it?"

Acting purely on protocol, Alyssa accepted the card and discreetly removed her arm from the woman's hand. She rose from the table. "Perhaps," she said vaguely. Right about the time she sprouted wings and learned to fly. With a tight smile, she gave a polite nod. "Enjoy your dinner."

Paulo took her arm and steered her toward the elevator. Alyssa trudged along, grateful to escape but still mortified and unable to focus.

"You've lost every ounce of color in your face," he said. After coming to a stop at the door, Paulo pushed the down button, staring at her with a frown. "I'm the first to admit my family is hellaciously unpleasant, but why would the mere mention of Tessa Harrison upset you so much?" With a muted ding, the doors slid open and Paulo led her inside.

Alyssa leaned weakly against the glass wall, ignoring the lights of Miami as the elevator began its descent down the side of the building. Maybe the bottom would swallow her up and ferry her directly to hell. That would be fitting.

"It's nothing," she said, avoiding his gaze.

"You're a lousy liar. You look like you've run into a ghost." He gently turned her face to meet his gaze, his eyes troubled. "What are you not telling me, Alyssa?"

She pulled her chin away and dropped her head back against the wall, exhausted from the encounter. She guessed the decision of how to finish the story had just been made for her. "Osten, the college that was supposed to save my reputation, kicked me out."

"You were expelled?" When she nodded, there was a pause before he asked the inescapable question. "Why?"

She slowly rolled her head along the wall to meet his gaze. "Because I got arrested again."

CHAPTER EIGHT

"DRINK this," Paulo said, breaking the silence.

He held out one of the two tumblers of bourbon in his hands and waited. As Alyssa sat on his living room couch, head resting against the back, eyes closed, he grew concerned by the lack of response. She hadn't said a word since the elevator. After her stunning declaration, he'd silently hustled her to the limousine, because Alyssa looked too strung out for questions.

Her face was white. Lips devoid of color. The circles under her eyes so well defined his gut clenched reflexively at the sight, a twinge pinching his chest.

It was damn disturbing.

But one glance at her and there had been no question he would bring her to his home. He didn't care about the run-in with his duplicitous brother and his ex-wife. Could even put aside hearing about the trust again. Everything was overpowered by the need to ease Alyssa's pain.

Finally, she sent him a weary expression and accepted the drink. "Aren't you tired of watching me fall apart and then shoving refreshments in my hand?"

Though relieved she'd recovered enough to speak, he watched to make sure she took a sip. He should have fed her first, but he suspected they both needed a bit of false courage.

"Aren't you going to say anything?" she said.

"I'm waiting for you to tell me what happened."

"I thought I already did."

He hated how she looked. Vulnerable. Defeated. As if someone had pulled the plug on her sassiness, sucking her spirit down the drain. The need to see the spunk return was fierce. Some color in her face wouldn't hurt either.

As he took a seat his hip brushed hers, sending a firestorm of signals that lit the deep, dark depths of his body. It wasn't a planned move, but Alyssa's cheeks turned pink. While that was a good thing, he pushed his need for her aside.

Now was not the time for a sensual road trip.

He fortified his resolve with a sip of bourbon. "You told me the beginning and the end. I want to hear the middle."

Staring at the drink in her hand, she rubbed her fingers along the glass, as if gathering her thoughts. It was a full minute before she spoke.

"For two years I attended Osten College. Every day I left my rundown neighborhood, taking several buses to reach the beautiful campus filled with beautiful people." Her gaze was unfocused, her voice distant, as if lost in the memories. "I tried to upgrade my wardrobe, just enough so I wouldn't stick out so much. It was hopeless, of course. But all I really wanted was to pretend my past didn't matter."

"That's understandable."

"Perhaps. But my mom kept telling me Osten was a mistake." With a rueful twist of her mouth, she went on. "That most people didn't believe in second chances. But I didn't want to listen." Threading her fingers through her hair, she dropped her voice a notch. "I was so sure she was wrong."

With a forced exhalation, Alyssa leaned forward and rested her elbows on her knees, her drink clutched in her hands. "Except while I was desperately trying to get my degree, to forget about my record and move on, when my classmates found out they made sure I never forgot."

Paulo would have endured a thousand meetings with his

brother just to wipe away her unhappy memories. "Life is rarely fair."

"And I *knew* that. But I was too pigheaded to accept it." She frowned, massaging her temple. "I had to push."

"How?" Paulo asked softly.

Her hand dropped to her knee. "Every year Osten arranges a parent-student luncheon. A horribly pompous affair, where the main topic of conversation is who has more money." With a pause, she stared down at her bourbon. "My sophomore year I volunteered to organize it."

"Why am I not surprised?" he said.

"My first official event." She let out an endearingly unladylike snort, but kept her attention on her drink, as if avoiding his gaze. "I spent hours putting it together because I wanted…" Her drawl died out as her fingertips went white against her glass. "I wanted to show them what I could do. To prove that I was more than a hick accent and a criminal past. That I had what it took to produce a glamorous social affair." And then she lifted her gaze to his, the gray eyes haunted, and his chest hitched again. "Ridiculous, right?"

Hit with the need to kiss those eyes closed, to heal her, Paulo gripped his glass instead. Touching her would be dangerous. "Not ridiculous. I busted my ass working for my dad for a similar reason." He laid his arm on the back of the couch. "Everyone wants their work appreciated."

"True," she said with a thoughtful nod. And then, after a sheepish glance, she looked back at her bourbon. "But I was tired of always wearing a waitress uniform to parties. And this was *my* event. So I wanted once, just this once, to wear something special." Her voice turned brittle. "And that's where my motivation runs amok."

She swiped a palm across her eyes, as if to collect herself, and then dropped her hand back to her drink. "I saved for months to buy a designer outfit. And I finally found the perfect one."

This time the wan smile was filled with guilt. "Pretty, but not too pretentious. I know it's stupid…" She dropped her gaze to her drink, swirling the amber liquid in her glass. "But when I tried it on in the dressing room it made me feel like one of those guests I was always serving. You know—" she lifted her glass "—classy. Chic. But still me." She tossed back the rest of her bourbon with a grimace. "Of course reality is always the kicker."

"I can see where this is going."

Her mouth turned grim. "Not so hard to figure it out."

"You didn't have enough."

"I was fifty dollars short."

She plunked her tumbler on the coffee table, her words escaping in a defeated rush. "God," she said. "I can't begin to describe how disappointed I was. The party was one day away, and while I sat in the dressing room, trying to figure out what to do…" Pressing her fingers to her mouth, she dropped her voice, the drawl growing thick. "I kept thinkin', '*What's one more time? If I never do it again after today, what difference will it make?*' And so I—"

Her voice broke, and she closed her eyes as if unable to go on. Another piece of Paulo's heart melted, and he ignored the alarms clanging in his head as he reached out, lacing his fingers with hers. He could feel the years of remorse in her grip on his hand.

When she turned to look at him, she'd recovered a bit. "I would have succeeded except the owner of the shop was at the party and recognized me." She let out a humorless laugh. "How's that for being served your just deserts?" Pausing, she fixed her gaze on Paulo, the smudge of purple beneath her eyes stark against her pale face. "And two years at Osten was nothing compared to the disgrace of being arrested at an event I'd organized."

The question in her eyes pulled him in as silent seconds passed into a full minute.

Paulo stared at her. He knew she was waiting for him to speak. Waiting for his reaction to her news. But he couldn't put it all together. Her soft skin, her delicate scent, and—far worse—the emotion in the squeeze of her fingers distracted him. The words wouldn't come.

And while he groped for a response Alyssa shot from the couch and crossed the room. "Don't you dare feel sorry for me," she said as turned to face him, folding her arms across her stomach. "Don't you get it? The real tragedy of this story?"

There were so many tragic parts he didn't know where to begin. But he knew what came next was important, and, as painful as it was to watch her suffer, he remained silent. Because he needed to know the answer. *Her* answer.

"It's not the poverty, or the way I was treated, or any of that." She tapped her chest with her fist, enunciating every word. "I wasn't strong enough to rise above it."

She began to pace with a frenetic energy. "I let a few superficial phonies matter. And I forgot the employer who took a risk on me. Forgot the pact I made with my mom. I let them both down. Let myself down." She clapped her hand to her forehead and came to a stop. "All over somethin' as dumb as an *outfit*," she said, as if after all these years she still couldn't quite believe what she'd done. She closed her eyes and leaned against the wall, her voice sounding weary. "Some epitaph that would make. 'Brought down by vanity and the lust for a designer dress.'"

Gutted by the look on her face, he felt the truth hit him like a lightning strike, blinding in its clarity. Slowly, he set down his drink. "I've been racking my brain trying to figure out why you work so hard," he said, watching her from across the room. "Why you push yourself." He stood and went to stand in front of her. He reached out to squeeze her fingers again. "It isn't going to be enough."

Confusion filled her face. "What?"

"Take it from someone who knows. Whatever you think you're trying to prove with your business, it won't be enough."

She drew in a wobbly breath, her hand clamped around his. "Without my business, I'm nothing more than a—"

With a press of his lips to hers, he cut off the sentence before she could complete it.

He had no idea what words she would have used to finish the statement. But, whatever was about to spill from her mouth, it wasn't true. Whatever she believed about herself, she was wrong. And, though he'd only meant to stop her, he allowed himself a moment to gather her lips deeper, to linger in the softness and the woodsy-sweet taste of bourbon.

After releasing her lips, he lifted his hand and gently cupped her jaw, but his tone was firm. "Everything you've been through has made you strong. Your business wouldn't be the success it is today without that trait."

He could see the rebuttal forming on her lips, and he cut her off, trying again. "The most respected people on this planet are those who can admit where they went wrong and go on to be better people. Just like you." The uncertainly in her face triggered a powerful protective urge, and his voice went low, insistent. "Everyone makes mistakes. No one is perfect. And while you're hell-bent on this life sentence you've appointed yourself—" hating the doubt in her eyes, he pulled her into his arms "—you're missing out on a future."

With a sigh, she leaned her forehead against his chest. "I'm not missing out. I'm just…" Her hands clutched his shirt, as if holding on for dear life. And with a sniff she went on, her voice fragile. "Just puttin' it on hold."

His heart slipped as he gathered her closer, like tires spinning out from beneath him. The momentum was frightening. And if he wasn't careful he'd crash for sure.

"Concentrate on who you are now, Alyssa," he said softly. "Let the past go."

As the minutes passed, he struggled to regain his equilibrium. But then he felt her fingers fumbling at his shirt, opening his buttons, and her lips landed on his skin. A kick of desire shot from his chest and landed with precision in his groin. Adding more weight to the unbalanced feeling.

His body demanded satisfaction, but he eased his hips away. "Alyssa," he said in warning. He couldn't do this now. No matter how much he wanted her. But she just popped the last button and looked up at him, her lids rimmed red. With a look of trust in her eyes that flattened him.

What had he done?

"No." He reached for her elbows. But she ignored him, pulling his shirt from his pants. Her hands slid down his chest as she brushed kisses along the open path. When her mouth landed on his abdomen, his muscles clenched in pleasure. "Alyssa, wait."

And then she dropped to her knees and nipped his erection through his pants.

Flames flared, and Paulo hissed, pulling her chin up. *"Don't,"* he said, staring down at her face. "You're tired. Feeling vulnerable." The frank passion in her luminous gray eyes was almost his undoing, but he felt wrung out. Too close to her. All the carefully constructed barriers he'd been fighting to keep in place had just received a potentially lethal hit. And being caught between the need to regain some distance and the maddening desire to consume her was pure hell. Ignoring the disappointment, he went on. "Now isn't the time."

"Yes...." Alyssa pushed his hips firmly against the wall and tugged open his zipper. "It is." After tugging down his pants, she palmed his shaft and ran her tongue from the base to the tip. The visceral hit was brutal, and a second hiss escaped his lips. He should push her away. But all he managed was to feel the sweat beading at his temples.

"I want you like this." Her words drawled against his skin. "And—" she licked his head "—don't stop before you're through." She lowered her mouth.

With a groan, Paulo arched his hips, delving deep. Alyssa moaned her approval, the sound vibrating around his erection. And, with her mouth boldly pleasuring him, she reached up to rake her nails down his chest, catching a flat nipple on the way.

Paulo shuddered and snapped.

Alyssa heard Paulo swear. He grabbed her wrists and pulled her up, whirling to pin her hands high on the wall above her head. Stunned, she stared at him. His shirt open, their bodies were pressed together from his bared chest down to his hips. His tone was low, harsh. "Why are you doing this?"

The words burst from her mouth. "Because I want you to stop holding back." She pressed her lips together, hating that she sounded so desperate.

Because now, after sharing her story, this man who knew all she'd done still looked at her the same way. *Still* had faith in her. A faith that scrubbed away the last traces of shame that clung to her like a tenacious stain.

And left her with a need that went beyond anything she'd felt before.

Yet every time he'd made love to her she'd known he was steering the event. Keeping his passion in check while she was reduced to a whimpering mess. And she wanted to drive him so crazy that he let out a shout. Like he did to her.

As she watched the internal battle in his eyes, tears pricked her lids. He'd had such a profound impact on her life. Touched her on so many levels. She was afraid that every time they'd made love it had been all about *her*.

And hadn't left a dent in his memory.

"I need you to lose control," she said.

Fury flared in his eyes as he thrust his erection against her belly, and the thrill had her body softening in response. His voice was rough, ragged. "You think I can control this?" He arched again, his shaft a band of steel. His eyes dropped to her breasts, mashed against him, and the tips puckered in response. "Your nipples beg when I walk in the room and it drives me insane."

They stared at each other, chests heaving. The demand for release intensified. With every brush against hard muscle, her body grew tighter.

Paulo lowered his mouth to her ear, and the growl in his voice dropped an octave. "Do you know how much I crave the feel of you coming against my lips?" Her breath caught, drowning in fire. He lifted his head, his mouth hovering over hers as he held her against the wall, his face angry. "Hearing your spicy Southern words egging me on?"

Alyssa cried out and crushed her lips to his, and their mouths melded in desperation, frantic. She wanted to touch him. To stroke his skin. Anywhere. *Everywhere.* To fuse them together. To hold on to this moment so it would last forever.

Frustrated by the impossibility, she pulled her hands free and clutched his face, nipping hard at his lower lip. Paulo shoved the hem of her skirt to her waist and lifted her, pinning her with his hips. With her legs wrapped around him, their mouths still locked, he dragged his thumbs across her nipples. The stab of pleasure was followed by a desperate thrust of his hips, and she savored his power, his passion. It was heaven. Nirvana. Supreme bliss.

This savage need they shared.

Then he shifted her higher, and Alyssa dragged his face to her breasts. She dropped her head back with a moan as Paulo feasted on her body through fabric, driving Alyssa to rock her hips. "Take me. *Now,*" she gasped.

His hands cupped her buttocks, and Paulo's mouth hungrily sought out her lips as he carried her down the hall to his bedroom.

"You know I can't resist you." He deposited her on the bed, yanking off his shirt and her panties, not bothering with his pants or her clothes. Fingers gripping her thighs, he spread her legs. She was overcome with the need to give him everything. All that she had.

This man who wanted her so badly, who saw her for who she was.

And liked it.

With no time for her to catch her breath, or for her body to gently adjust to his, he drove his shaft deep.

Paulo heard Alyssa's gasp and began a demanding rhythm, a mating that was pure possession. It was wild, unruly, bordering on too much, too soon. He knew he should slow down, let her body acclimatize to his, but he couldn't. Because she hitched her knees higher, hot, wet, begging him for more, her skin damp. And with every reach of his hips he went a little deeper. Surged higher.

Straightening his arms, he arched his back to better angle his hips between her legs. "Alyssa," he groaned.

The muscles in his chest and biceps tensed as he plunged deep, again and again. The feel of his body joined with hers drove him forward. This terrible, destructive desire to imprint himself on her. To leave a mark and brand her his forever.

The room filled with the slick sound of skin on skin, the smell of sweat. The erotic sensations worked their magic, softening her, until Paulo buried himself to the base of his erection. "Oh, God," he breathed. But still…it wasn't enough.

Damn it. Why wasn't it enough?

Agitated, he clasped her shoulders to hold her in place as his movements grew rough, reckless. He felt feverish. Burning with the fire that was consuming him. Tearing him down and building him back up. Hating the loss of control.

And loving it.

He stared down at her, and their gazes locked. "Is this what you wanted?" he said hoarsely.

"Yes." She should look frightened, as disturbed as he felt. Instead, there was only ecstasy. *"Yes."*

With a guttural groan the last of his reserve splintered, and his hips bucked madly. Eager, throaty gasps escaped her with every thrust. Arching her neck in pleasure, Alyssa braced her hands on the headboard, inflaming him with her provocative words. The bed thumped against the wall. He was desperate to end the agony. To satisfy this need that was devouring him bit by bit. Bite by bite. Taking pieces of him he knew he'd never get back.

And then she came undone.

With a final violent thrust, Paulo threw back his head with a shout. Alyssa clutched his body, holding him deep inside her as the powerful orgasm released its hold on him, the magnitude crushing in its painful pleasure.

Alyssa woke at midnight to the sound of distant thunder and the feel of Paulo's body spooned against her back, his arms around her waist. A storm was approaching. She could hear the gusts of wind, the rustling of tree branches, and their occasional scrape against his bedroom window.

Between the grueling discussion about her past and their explosive lovemaking, she had been mentally and physically whipped. Paulo had fixed a simple meal and brought it to her in bed. Once they'd eaten, she'd been incapable of anything beyond the need for sleep. He had pulled her close, the tenderness in his touch like a healing salve, and she'd drifted off, at peace. And full of something she hadn't felt in years…

Optimism. Hope for the future.

Ten years of being petrified she'd let her image slip—saying the wrong thing, *doing* the wrong thing—was a grinding wear and tear to her psyche that had slowly eroded her strength. She was exhausted from the sheer effort of keeping up her guard. But with Paulo she didn't have to measure her every word, her every response.

In bed or out.

And the happiness was so new, so unexpected, she wanted to cling to it for as long as she could. She didn't want to waste precious time with Paulo engaged in an internal debate about the choices she'd made since her arrest. That could come later.

Much, much later.

A streak of lightning lit the room, and Paulo shifted. "You're still here." His words hummed against her ear. "I thought I'd wake up alone again."

Raindrops began to splatter against the window, and she snuggled closer to Paulo, his king-size bed warm and inviting. "I'm too comfortable."

"Good," he said as he tightened his arms around her waist. "Because the whole point of the morning after is to indulge in more of what went on the night before."

"I don't know if I want to repeat all of tonight."

"Mmm," he murmured. "How about just the best parts?" he said with a sexy rumble.

A second smile touched her lips. But despite the incredible memories his words had resurrected, the awkward moment with his brother and ex-wife flashed in her mind. Obviously that was one part of the evening *he* didn't wish to repeat. He hadn't broached the subject of their encounter with his family, and she was positive he wouldn't bring it up. Watching his tight face during the encounter had been difficult.

Alyssa absently rubbed her fingers against his arm, the rough hair coarse. "I'm sorry about the run-in with Marcos and Bianca."

A few moments passed before he replied, "It doesn't matter."

Her fingers stalled on his arm. He'd been nonchalant about the subject before, and this discussion was never going to be easy, but surely, after everything they had just been through he would feel more at ease talking to her now?

"It had to have hurt when she left you for Marcos." When he didn't respond, she went on. "And your brother's actions must have hurt your relationship with him, too."

His harsh scoff came out close to her ear. "The only thing Marcos and I ever shared was an unfriendly competition at work."

Alyssa twisted in his arms to look up at him. "You two were never close?"

Another jagged flash of lightning lit his face, complete with a Rochester-esque scowl that would've had Jane Eyre swooning in her shoes. When the accompanying grumble of thunder finally arrived, Alyssa waited for the sound to pass, and then his reply. But the silence was only broken by the increasing force and frequency of pattering rain.

Paulo rolled onto his back, his left arm still beneath her waist, and finally spoke. "Six months before I left the business, I approached my father about creating a boutique line within the company." It wasn't an answer to her question, but Alyssa waited, knowing the story was important. "I wanted to take our older, smaller hotels and renovate them. Restore them to their original designs." The light was dim, but as he stared up at the ceiling she could just make out the frown on his mouth. "And I wanted the Samba to be the first. But, as usual, Marcos and I…" He hesitated before going on. "We disagreed about the idea."

She sensed those disagreements had been heated. "So what happened?"

"My father had a stroke, throwing the company into chaos. And then, four months later, while Marcos and I were still arguing about my proposal, Dad died from complications."

The story was recounted with as much emotion as it took to read a grocery list. But the loss of his father must have been tough. "I'm sorry."

His reply was wooden. "Don't be."

She couldn't tell if he was glad his dad was dead, or missed him terribly, or any of the countless variations in between. And his refusal to talk was daunting. Ignoring the pang of disappointment, she boldly pressed on. Persistence was her only ally. "If Marcos and Bianca's relationship doesn't bother you, why are you refusing to talk to your brother about the trust?"

The frown grew deeper. "Because there's nothing to talk about."

Her forehead crinkled with concern. "You don't expect me to believe that, do you?"

"I don't want the money."

Alyssa propped her head on her hand. "Why not?"

The fingers beneath her hip growing tight. "Because I don't need it."

"But don't you feel an obligation to honor your father's last wishes?"

With his free hand, Paulo raked his hair from his forehead. And as she waited the frustration grew. One night of feeling unbelievably close to him had rocked the very foundation of her world. She was different. Irrevocably altered. Hadn't it changed anything for him? Hadn't he felt the slightest shift in their relationship?

Feeling an overwhelming need to press the issue, she went on. "Why won't you answer the question?"

Paulo pulled his hand from her waist. "It's been a long day. And we're both tired." His voice was low, laced with fatigue. He rolled over to face the wall. "Get some sleep, Alyssa."

She stared at his back, listening to the sound of the rain pummel the window, confused. And hurt. After letting every ounce of her soul pour out for him to see, he still didn't feel comfortable talking to her.

With an ominous feeling, a massive caution light was blinking in her brain. Flashing brighter than the lightning that streaked across the night sky. And if she were smart she'd start paying attention. Problem was, when it came to Paulo nothing about her was smart. And she realized she'd gone and made another mistake. Another *horrible* mistake.

She'd fallen in love with Paulo Domingues.

CHAPTER NINE

AT 2:00 a.m., Paulo leaned against the wall of the patio outside his bedroom, staring at the shifting lights in his pool. The storm had passed, leaving the smell of damp earth and a heavy humidity, and it pressed in on him. Despite the rain, it was still hot. And the temperature, the black night, along with the moisture in the air, all combined until it became a wet, oppressive box. Inside the house, it was air-conditioned and cool, but Alyssa still slept in his bed, and he didn't want to wake her.

He felt bruised. Battered. And beat up.

When he'd brought her to his home he hadn't counted on being completely gutted by her story. The unbearable need to put her world right. Much less the alarming look of absolute trust she'd given him. And when she'd finally unleashed her wild side, a hellcat in bed, it had knocked his control out of the park.

Once that wall had been breached, he was powerless to stop it.

Restless, he crossed the small porch and leaned his elbows on the rail, frowning as he watched the pool light shimmy, flickering blue ghosts against the trees. He should have ended their affair when she'd continued to question him about his family. But he couldn't seem to bring himself to do it. Instead, like an idiot, he'd told her about the argument with Marcos. Granted, it was a diluted version of the story—like watered-down Scotch, it didn't sting as much going down—but he'd thought it would satisfy her. But it hadn't been enough.

Would probably never be enough.

And the more he gave, the more Alyssa would want. She was tough. Tenacious. With her childhood, she'd had to be. But as she'd continued to push and push, the warier he'd become…and the more she'd sounded like Bianca.

Stifling him. Cutting off his air just as surely as a constraining wedding ring around his finger. Over the course of his year of marriage Bianca had grown pushier, needier, and that circle of gold had grown tighter, until it had felt like he was choking.

And he was choking now.

He sank into the patio chair and scrubbed his face in frustration.

From the moment he'd met Alyssa he'd been in over his head. What he needed now was space. Room to catch his breath. Things had gotten out of hand and way too intense. It was time to back off for a bit. With any luck, by putting a little distance between them and this evening, he could ease them back into the simple affair this was meant to be.

And if that wasn't enough for Alyssa, then it would be time to move on.

Three days later Alyssa sat on her couch, a shot of whiskey in her hand. The publicity from the wedding reception had taken on a life of its own, and her cellular had been ringing non-stop. And thank goodness, too, because she was left with nothing but work to keep her busy.

After the life-altering evening with Paulo, he'd told her to see Charles with any problems and then left for Boca Raton to check out a hotel for sale. This afternoon he'd called to ask her to meet him at Nick's club tomorrow. The conversation had been short, with Paulo avoiding every question she'd asked.

With a sigh, she tucked her bare feet beneath her. Things

were going so well at work there was little doubt Paulo now had complete faith in her abilities as an event planner. She'd reached her goal. Secured her dream job. And she'd ruined it all by falling in love with a man who didn't do wedding rings anymore.

Love.

Damn, girl. Don't pretend you didn't see this parade of pain coming.

Her breath whooshed out in a hiss, and she traced the furrow between her brows. He'd offered a few weeks of fun and sex, and now she wanted more. And there was a vast void that spanned the space between a casual fling and forever.

A sharp knock was followed by a jingle of metal. There was only one person who had a key to her apartment.

Her mother entered and spotted her on the couch. "Oh, here you are." She closed the door and tossed the keys on a chair. "I dropped by the Samba to find out your plans for dinner…" Her gaze fell to Alyssa's glass, and her movements grew slow, as if sensing the negative vibes. "I think I'll join you." She headed into the kitchen and grabbed a glass from the cupboard, returning to plop down next to Alyssa. "So, what's wrong?"

Alyssa rubbed her glass with her fingers. "Work has been busy, and I wanted to relax." As she summoned the energy to tell the truth, she watched her mother pick up the almost full bottle of whiskey from the coffee table and pour herself a shot.

"It's six o'clock and you're already home." Her mom narrowed her eyes, her gaze dropping back to Alyssa's hand. "You're not turning into an alchy, are you?" Without waiting for an answer, she plunked the bottle on the table. "I think you need to slow down. Lord knows, the pace you keep would drive me to drink." She brushed at her bright blond feathery bangs, frowning at her own glass. "Though I'd prefer a beer to this stuff. Anyway, my friend told me about this new rehab clinic down on—"

"Mom," she said, unable to take it anymore, "I'm not an alcoholic."

Her mother settled deeper into the sofa, as if preparing for a long story. "So what's the problem?"

"I slept with Paulo Domingues."

"Lyssa." Her mother sat up, twisting to face her on the couch. Alyssa braced for her reaction, and after a moment of shocked silence her mom reached out to touch her hand. "I'm so proud of you."

Flabbergasted, Alyssa rested her glass on her jean clad knee. "After five years of working hard to build my business, you're *proud* of me for sleeping with a client?"

"You took a risk. You put yourself out there." She gave Alyssa's hand a final pat. "Good for you."

Alyssa briefly closed her eyes. Not so good for her. She'd taken a risk and fallen hard. Her voice went low, and she asked the question that had been swirling in her mind since Paulo had left town. "How am I supposed to work with him now?"

"Well, if you quit, would it be horrible of me if I dated his manager?" As Alyssa absorbed the news, her mother tried to look innocent while sipping her whiskey. "Charles asked me out to dinner." For the first time ever, Alyssa saw her mother blush. "He's really very sweet."

Sweet. Charles. *Sweet?* Alyssa blinked, trying to picture it, and then finally gave up. Some things were just beyond her comprehension. And, since her mother was one of them, perhaps the two were meant to be.

Unlike her and Paulo. A piercing fear robbed her of her breath.

"I reckon that's enough about me. What do *you* want?" her mother said.

The impossible, apparently. "I want Paulo," Alyssa said. "I love him."

"Then go after him, honey."

"He doesn't want commitment."

"Fiddle-faddle. Men don't know what they want. It's up to us to show them."

Alyssa sent her a wan smile. She'd inherited her mother's stubbornness, and her accent, but she didn't come close to touching her confidence. As time ticked by, Alyssa couldn't think of a response, and a sober look slowly washed over her mother's face.

"I was too young to be a parent," her mom said. "And I know I made mistakes."

Alyssa went still, stunned by the expression and the words. Her mother rarely admitted to anything. She preferred to pretend all was well even when things were falling apart, which had been constant when Alyssa was little. "It's okay, Mom."

"No, it's not."

"You did the best you could."

"Maybe. I'm real sorry my choices made your life so difficult." She shook her head, her massive hoop earrings swinging. "But I never regretted having you." The fine lines around her eyes eased as her expression softened. "That's all I want for you, baby. A life without regrets."

A lump formed in Alyssa's throat, and she swallowed hard, trying to clear it.

"So," her mom said, the easy-breezy smile returning to her face. "How 'bout I swing by the Samba tomorrow and take you to lunch?"

Amused by the lightning change, Alyssa sent her a tiny smile. "I'd like that."

"Good." Her mother pushed up off the couch. "Now, while you think of a way to straighten out your boyfriend, your momma is gonna make us some dinner."

Watching her go, Alyssa slumped against the couch and twirled a lock of hair in her finger.

A life without regrets.

It sounded good, but where did she go from here? Just thinking about her feelings for Paulo left her lungs tight and a sick feeling in her stomach. And after tossing and turning all night the only thing she knew for sure was that she couldn't give up. But how did you reach a man who refused to talk about his feelings?

With the sound of pots clinking in the kitchen, Alyssa listened to her mother singing a country song. Despite their problems, she could always count on her mom. Her love. And her loyalty. And, although Alyssa's childhood had been difficult, there was one thing she was beginning to truly understand: being wealthy didn't necessarily make it any easier.

She knew Paulo's time at his father's business had been tough. And if his family's only concern was money and success, maybe communication wasn't a priority at his home? Perhaps he didn't talk about the painful parts because he'd never been shown how?

Despite his horrendous treatment by Marcos and Bianca, it was his father that he refused to discuss. And maybe, just maybe, if she learned the secret to their relationship, convinced him to accept the money and get past whatever was eating at him, it might allow him to let her in, too. Outside of Nick, who was probably too loyal to share the truth, the only other person who might be willing to discuss the matter with her was Bianca.

Alyssa dropped her gaze to her cellular, resting on the coffee table. When she'd opened the email from Paulo's ex-wife, requesting her help again, Alyssa had planned on deleting it, but never got the chance. There was no telling what Tessa Harrison had said to Bianca, and Alyssa dreaded the thought of dealing with her plastic smile again, but it was one way to learn about Paulo's father. A long shot, maybe. And, considering how Paulo might feel about it, definitely risky. But she was used to both.

Alyssa twisted her whiskey glass on her knee, eyeing her phone with apprehension. When he'd called today, Paulo wouldn't even elaborate on why he wanted to meet her at the club. Somehow she didn't think it was to profess an undying love for her.

With a sigh, she reached for her cellular and began her search for Bianca's number.

Bianca Domingues was the only woman Alyssa knew who made a white tennis skirt and a ponytail look chic.

"I can't thank you enough for helping me, Alyssa," Bianca said.

Her kindness was surprising, but so was Bianca's request for help with her *wedding anniversary.*

Alyssa's apprehension had climbed higher at the news, and she'd hesitated. But after a few seconds of intense deliberation she'd proceeded anyway. Because, although she planned on trying to learn a little about Paulo's dad, her arrangement with Bianca wasn't personal. It was purely a business deal.

And if anyone would understand that, it was Paulo.

After questioning Bianca for half an hour on the phone, Alyssa had landed on the perfect theme. When she'd arrived at her home today to present it, Bianca had graciously served up refreshments in her manicured backyard, the view overlooking the tennis courts and the Atlantic beyond.

"The country club has been marvelously accommodating on such short notice," Bianca said. "But their ideas were a little—" she wrinkled her nose, shifting the sprinkle of freckles on her sun dappled face, red hair gleaming in the light "—ordinary," she finished. Her eyes lit with excitement as she leaned forward. "I absolutely adore your idea for a theme."

It was impossible to hold back a smile at her infectious enthusiasm. "I'm glad you're pleased." Alyssa took a sip of her iced tea before going on. "We were lucky the vendor's casino tables were available. Passing out chips to your guests and indulging in a Monte Carlo fantasy will certainly be different."

Bianca's smile grew bigger. "Marcos loved the gaming clubs during our honeymoon there."

Which hardly matched Alyssa's impression of the man. Then again, nothing was turning out as expected. After all the time she'd spent fretting about meeting the woman again, it had turned out to be a wasted expenditure of angst.

"Up until now, we always left town for our anniversary." Bianca's smile slowly faded. "After all the vile things the newspapers printed after we married…" She blushed, and with a delicate shrug abandoned the sentence. "But this year Marcos has been working so hard, has been gone so much, I decided at the last minute it was time to celebrate at home." Bianca squarely met Alyssa's gaze, as if daring her to question the decision.

But Alyssa understood the need to stop running from the past. "I'll finalize the plans with the vendor today."

Bianca reached out to touch Alyssa's hand, her eyes full of gratitude. "Thank you," she said. "I know I'm paying you for your time, but if there is anything I can do for you—anything at all—please let me know."

Suspicion snaked along Alyssa's stomach. The same sensation she'd had when she talked to Nick at the track. She couldn't shake the feeling Paulo's ex-wife was trying to tell her something. Twisting her glass on the table, Alyssa gathered her courage. "I was hoping you could tell me a little about Paulo's father."

Bianca looked surprised at the question. After a moment, she picked up her drink and paused, studying her glass with great care. "Ricardo was my godfather. He was a wonderful man and very generous to me." She took a sip before going on. "But he wasn't overly affectionate toward his sons. And he was particularly hard on them after they joined the company." She set her glass carefully on the table and went on. "Most would probably say he was too hard. But I believe he had the best of intentions. Running Domingues International is not for the faint of heart." Pride crept across her face. "Marcos is very good at what he does."

After another pause, Bianca reached for a canapé. "Which brings me to a second favor I'd like to ask of you. You seem to have captured Paulo's attention," Bianca said. Alyssa's eyes widened a fraction, and Bianca sent her a deliberate look. "I was hoping you could convince him to come to my party."

Blinking back her surprise, Alyssa sat back in her chair. Despite Paulo's insistence that his brother and ex-wife were welcome to each other, she doubted that extended to Paulo attending their anniversary party. "I don't think he would listen to me," she said truthfully.

Hors d'oeuvres in her hand, Bianca's face hardened with determination. "I really want to see Paulo put an end to this ridiculous vendetta. Marcos has suffered enough."

Marcos has suffered? She watched Bianca daintily nibble on a cracker topped with crab salad. How could the woman say that with a straight face? Because from where Alyssa was sitting—admittedly a position that was starting to feel like complete ignorance—Marcos wasn't the one who had suffered.

"Did Paulo leave the family business because of you and your husband's marriage?" Alyssa said.

Bianca coughed and wiped her mouth with a napkin. With a frown, she finally lowered her hand to the table. "Paulo didn't tell you?" Heat crept up Alyssa's cheeks, which must have been answer enough. "Of course he didn't." Bianca leaned back and crossed her arms. "He hasn't changed a bit. Even after a year of marriage, I never could get him to share anything with me, either."

The news was hard to hear, and Alyssa felt like a lead weight was growing in her chest.

The redhead continued. "It was never made public knowledge, but when my godfather died he left the business to Marcos. That was when Paulo left."

Alyssa stared at Bianca, shocked by the news. Dissed by his own father. What kind of man favored one son over another? And why should she have to learn everything about him off the internet and from his ex-wife?

Bianca seemed oblivious to Alyssa's shock. "Paulo was so driven to outdo Marcos and prove himself to his dad," she went on. "I could have been happy, despite his grungy clothes and workaholic ways, if he had simply opened up." Bianca's face turned pensive, and profoundly…sad. "But finally I accepted the fact that he could never learn to love me the way I loved him."

The lead weight in Alyssa's chest grew heavier. This was not the story she'd come to hear. Nor was it the story the newspapers had told. Fashion snob, maybe, but the cold, calculating woman was nowhere to be found.

"And then my godfather had a stroke—" Bianca's voice broke a little, and she cleared her throat before she continued. "I was so unhappy, and Paulo was no help." Her gaze drifted to the turquoise waters, hurt evident in her expression. "Every time I tried to discuss it with him, he'd turn his back on me."

The words struck with the force of a twenty-foot tidal wave, and the blood slowly seeped from Alyssa's face, robbing her of the power of speech. She remembered the sight of his back and the feeling it produced. Heart pounding, Alyssa desperately reached for her iced tea. She took a tasteless sip, struggling to get it down, only half listening as Bianca went on.

"But Marcos was wonderfully supportive. And as we dealt with Ricardo's illness, we grew closer." Bianca looked at Alyssa again. "Over time, I realized I'd married the wrong brother."

Alyssa felt ill, the nausea growing with every passing second, and she *so* didn't want to throw up here.

"I'm sorry," Bianca said softly. "I know how frustrating it is to love Paulo and not be able to reach him."

Alyssa didn't want to hear anymore. Didn't want to discuss Paulo with Bianca. She needed to escape. Her hands fumbled as she reached for her purse. "I should be going now. I have an evening appointment," she said as she stood.

In truth, she had to meet Paulo at Nick's club.

How ironic.

"I'll call you after I've made the final arrangements with the vendor," Alyssa said with a tight smile, and then took off across the closely cropped lawn.

She managed to get about five feet before the woman spoke again. "Alyssa?" Bianca said.

Alyssa's heart dropped. There would be no escape yet. She stopped and slowly turned to face the lady.

"Tessa Harrison told me she contacted a *Miami Insider* reporter about you," Bianca said. Alyssa's heart sank further, settling to her toes like a stone as Bianca continued. "Your past is none of my business, so I haven't discussed it with anyone." Compassion filled her face. "But I thought you deserved to know."

Staring at her blankly, Alyssa managed to mutter her thanks, and then headed off again, her mind reeling from the double dose of bad news.

But the truth about Paulo's marriage was more disturbing than a vague threat of possible exposure in a tabloid magazine. Dazed, she made her way toward Bianca's driveway, and then she heard the distant sound of the surf. On impulse, she slipped off her pumps and carried them, cutting through the sea oats on a well-used path.

Feet sinking in the sand, she aimlessly wandered along the beach, lost in thought. The marriage itself hadn't bothered her. Plenty of people made the commitment, only to have it fall apart. Divorce didn't ruin a person for relationships forever.

When he'd insisted he didn't make promises, Alyssa had

assumed it was because he was wary of being hurt again. But ratcheting up her torture meter to intolerable levels was the news he'd hurt Bianca first. Repeatedly. Treating his wife the same way he was treating Alyssa now.

With a heavy heart, Alyssa climbed the steps of a boardwalk running along a public beach, her legs tired from trudging through sand. An empty bench nestled under the cool cover of a palm tree was too tempting to pass, and she collapsed onto the seat, gaze fixed on the sunlight glistening off the water. She smelled salt. She felt the warm breeze.

But would she ever feel normal again?

A couple wandered by and settled onto a towel to soak up the sun, making goo-goo eyes at each other. The sight of people in love, enjoying their life, had never bothered her before.

She let out a heavy sigh. Life had been so simple before Paulo coaxed her into an affair. She'd been satisfied with days full of nothing but her business. But now…

A Pandora's box of discontent had been thrown wide open, and there was no going back.

And it wasn't as if the thought of strolling along the beach *alone* was appealing. She wanted Paulo with her. Forever. Alyssa gripped the edge of the wooden seat.

He'd turned his back on Bianca, just as he had her.

She pressed her lids closed. But she couldn't simply take Bianca's word about their less than ideal marriage. It wouldn't be fair. There were two sides to every relationship story, and she needed to know Paulo's.

And, no matter how much he didn't want to discuss it, when she met up with him tonight she had every intention of finding out.

"Do you always park the Ducati on the sidewalk entryway?"

At the sound of Alyssa's voice, Paulo turned from the rail lining the dance floor of the cavernous club fashioned after an old warehouse. Neon lights pulsed in time with the music. People filled every nook and cranny. But in jeans and a pink blouse, hair pulled back in a matching scarf, Alyssa was more beautiful than every woman in the room. His body went incredibly hard and inexplicably soft, all at the same time.

"The security guys at the door watch her for me," he finally said.

She lifted a brow dryly. "I hope you at least pay them for babysitting."

His lips twitched, and she sent him a tiny smile as they stared at each other.

He had done what he'd set out to do, spending the last two days buried in his review of the numbers at the Ocean Inn. Taking a breather. Clearing his head. Now he was just glad to be back, struck with the urgent need to hold her again.

Not wanting to break the spell, he silently took her hand and led her onto the now dimly lit dance floor, pulling her close as a slow song started up. "It's good to have you back in my arms," he said. He leaned in to inhale her floral scent.

"I've been waiting to talk to you."

"Talk?" Fingers flexing against her hips, he brought her flush against him, and a dark look flickered in Alyssa's eyes. Pleased with her reaction, he leaned in for a kiss.

Alyssa stopped him with a hand to his chest. "Look, Romeo," she said dryly. "You can't just waltz back into my life and start putting the moves on me."

He shifted his gaze to her hair and rubbed a silky lock between his fingers, forcing the conversation back to a light tone. "I don't think I should be compared to Romeo. His plan was flawed. Worse, he fell for a lady who made poor choices, too." He hiked a brow. "What kind of woman stabs herself through the heart?"

"A woman devastated by the loss of love." She stared at him, and the pause stretched as the blood grew heavy in his veins. "Because, unlike us, Romeo and Juliet were *really* involved."

Paulo frowned at her serious expression. He might not want anything permanent, but he wouldn't pretend their time together wasn't special. His movements slowed until their feet were barely shifting on the floor. The sensual slide of thigh on thigh left a smoldering ache in its wake, and his grip on her hip grew tight. "We've spent an extraordinary amount of time together for two people who aren't involved."

Alyssa's chin rose stubbornly. "Time together at work doesn't count," she said. The pink tinge to her cheeks brought out her gray eyes, and the way she hitched her breath had her lovely chest heaving erotically against him.

Damn if he didn't want her again.

And he wouldn't let her dismiss their sizzling chemistry so easily. He lowered his mouth close to hers and arched his body against hers, nearly groaning out loud at the instant agonizing pleasure. "How about when you pushed me against the wall of my living room?" His voice was husky from the memory. "Does that count?"

Shifting from pink to red, her face lost a little of its confidence. "No, the sex doesn't count either."

Frustration surged. "The hell it doesn't," he growled, and took her lips with his.

One hand securing her neck, he slaked his mouth across hers, while the other hand clutched her buttock, pressing his erection firmly against her. He wanted her to *feel* his powerful reaction. Because, despite her words, it was a reaction they shared. Her lips went soft, compliant, and the desire expanded until it devoured him.

Alyssa ripped her mouth away. "Stop." She pushed against him. He stared at her as he fought for breath, his chest heaving, his heart thundering beneath her hand. "You can't seduce your way out of this conversation," she said.

Paulo stepped back, raking an aggravated hand through his hair. He wanted to have this talk about as much as he wanted to contract a deadly disease. And certainly not with an audience.

He took her hand. "Let's take this to the VIP room."

CHAPTER TEN

As THEY threaded through the crowd, Alyssa's body still vibrated from the scorching kiss. It was hopeless. Being in love made her reaction to the man unbearable. But, as painful as it had been to pull away, she couldn't let him distract her.

Blinded by nerves, she followed along as he led her up a metal staircase along the far wall, across a landing, and into a small room with leather furniture. A massive picture window overlooked the dance floor below.

Paulo rounded the corner bar. "Would you like a cocktail?"

"Club soda, please."

"Sure you don't need a splash of something in it?"

Alyssa took a seat and crossed her legs, bracing for the discussion. "Quite sure."

He poured her a drink. "So what do you want to talk about, Alyssa?"

"Us." He cocked his head, waiting, and she went on. "You know every gory detail about me, yet I know very little about you." She'd *thought* she did. But today had proved just how mistaken she'd been. And it cut to the quick. "I'm not happy with how one-sided our relationship has become."

He carefully set the bottle of club soda down, a line between his eyebrows as he studied her. "You were on board with my conditions from the start."

"The conditions that our relationship would be based on work and sex?" She'd been stupid enough to think that would make it *easier*. Heaven help her, how wrong could she get? "Your plan also allowed for a couple of weeks, at best."

Frowning, he dropped his hand to his side. "Maybe I've changed my mind about the time limit."

Hope swelled, but she ignored it. She linked her fingers at the end of her knee. "An affair that lasts an eternity can't replace a relationship that's deep enough to have an honest discussion."

As he crossed the floor with her club soda, his tone went firm. "There's nothing to discuss." With a guarded expression, he handed her the drink. Heat flashed in his eyes as their fingers brushed.

Skin tingling, her stomach took a free fall in desperate need of a parachute. Good Lord, the man could befuddle her brain with a simple touch. Clutching the glass, she held his gaze. But it was time to get to the meat of the matter. "I picked up a new event today." Confusion swept across his face, and Alyssa took a sip before going on, regretting it wasn't stronger. "Bianca hired me." As his expression slowly fell, her heart rate rose.

Courage, Alyssa. Courage.

"I'm helping with her anniversary plans," she finished.

With a stunned face, he stared at her, his voice gruff with disbelief. "You're organizing my brother's anniversary party?"

She worried her lower lip, alarm sending her heart rate soaring higher. "Not organizing it, no." She adjusted her scarf with shaky fingers. "I'm helping her with the theme."

Gaze fixed on hers, he looked at her as if he'd never seen her before. "Is this your way of manipulating me into discussing my family?"

Her heart stumbled and fell, getting bruised in the process. "Manipulating you?" Though shocked, hurt by his words, Alyssa managed to tip her chin in defiance. "No honor among thieves, you mean?" When he kept silent, she went on, despite the painful wound. "This is my way of learning more about you. Because *you* refuse to be honest enough to tell me."

A dark look flitted through his eyes before they went cold, glittering. His voice dripped with accusation. "My ex-wife is none of your business."

Alyssa froze, staggered by the callous words and frigid delivery. She had hoped for an opening for a frank conversation. But there was none. Only an insult and a harsh reminder she had overstepped the boundaries he'd placed on their relationship.

She bit back the bubble of a hysterical laugh, the absurdity of the moment not lost on her. "I guess she's my business now."

White lines of anger etched firmly around his mouth, he said, "And I'm sure my brother appreciates the use of your skills on his behalf." And then, almost as an afterthought, he went on with a scoff, "No doubt Bianca will be pleased with your work, too."

Marcos. Just like at the restaurant, his anger was directed mainly at Marcos. So who was he mad at most? Bianca, for walking out on him, or his brother for replacing him? Hearing about Paulo's behavior during his marriage, watching his reaction now, she knew it was the latter. Heart growing heavy, she finally touched on the worst discovery of all. The thought she'd been avoiding all day. She'd hoped he'd simply buried the pain, because the memory of being hurt by an old love she could fight.

But if Paulo was simply incapable of love…?

And, as much as she hated to, she had to admit all the evidence was pointing in that direction. Which meant the outlook for a future with Paulo was growing dimmer and dimmer. She closed her eyes against the mounting pile of anguish, trying to focus on her original goal.

After swallowing hard, she met his gaze. "I think Bianca

would be more pleased if you accepted your father's money. And ended the feud with your brother," she added.

The look he shot her was sharp. "Then perhaps she shouldn't have dumped me for him."

Her palms grew damp, but she forced herself to remain calm. Because she had to speak her mind. She'd seen the pain on Bianca's face. It was real. Alyssa knew leaving hadn't been easy for her. "Bianca isn't perfect. No one is, as you so prophetically told me yourself. But at least she tried to make the marriage work. Truthfully." She lifted her chin at his budding expression of disbelief. "I think you drove her away."

Paulo stepped closer to the couch. The skeptical fury in his eyes as he stared down at her was a force to behold, and his voice was harsh. "And just what the hell would you know about it?"

She blinked back the hurt, because she knew plenty now. The expression on his face as he froze her out had been chilling. And his thunderous look right now was shattering. "Actually, I know quite a lot," she said unsteadily. And what she'd learned matched Bianca's account, not his. "We had a very illuminating conversation about you."

"She used me."

"I don't believe that."

"You're going to take my ex-wife's version of the truth over mine?"

"When it corresponds with my own version of the truth?" she said. "Yes."

"And what *is* your version of the truth?"

He wouldn't like what she had to say this time either, but she said it anyway. If any hope remained for the two of them, no matter how tiny, it had to come through a ruthless look at his past. An *honest* look. "That you hold back from the people in your life. From me. From your brother. And at one time from your wife. You may have married Bianca, but you never tried to make it work."

He returned to the wall and propped a shoulder against the glass, sarcasm oozing from his voice. "Is that what you think?"

"That's what I think."

"At least I have a life. *Friends.*"

Alyssa ignored the jab. "Friends that don't require much from you."

His eyebrows reached for the roof. "Now you're attacking my loyalty to Nick?"

She shook her head in frustration. "I didn't say you weren't loyal. You are. But Nick doesn't make any demands on you. An aren't-we-good-buddies friendship allows you the freedom to give what you want, when you want, and nothing more." The conclusions she'd reached as he'd treated her so callously came tumbling out, her fingers crushing her glass. "You want a lover for your bed, an easygoing friend, but you don't want anything that resembles a deep relationship because—"

"I tried commitment once," he said with a scowl. "And I hated it."

"You didn't try. It was just a ring on your finger and a legal paper filed in your office. And you don't want commitment because it's all about *Paulo*. You want to choose when, what, and how much, if any, you'll share, and—"

"You know what?" he said, cutting her off again as he pushed away from the glass wall. "I didn't sign on for this." He thrust an agitated hand through his hair. "And I have no intention of competing with your idea of the perfect boyfriend. I didn't want to compete with my wife's idea of a perfect husband, and I sure as *hell* got tired of competing for the role of perfect son."

"Don't you get it?" She shot off the couch and crossed the floor to stand in front of him, her tumbler clutched in her hand. "That's what the Samba is all about. You're *still* competing with Marcos." Why was he so blind to the truth? Why couldn't he see it? "But now it's just a pitiful competition for the attentions of a ghost." Surely somewhere, buried beneath all that anger, there must be pain. Dying to get him to let her in—just a little crevice that might lead to more—she reached out to touch his arm as she tried to steady her drawling voice. "Sooner or later you're going to have to let that go, Paulo." Her voice dropped low. "Because you can't win the approval of a dead man."

He pulled his arm from her hand and turned to face the glass. She was left looking at a familiar image. His back. Devastated, she stood still, feeling empty, drained and defeated.

He'd made her laugh, teased her and flirted shamelessly. But he'd also treated her with great tenderness. That proved he was capable of caring, didn't it? Or maybe she was just hoping that was true. Her heart, already bleeding, bled a little more. "Is this really who you want to be?" she croaked hoarsely. "Someone so cold?"

His voice was devoid of emotion. "Are you done?"

She closed her eyes against the pressure of hot tears.

My God, I'm being dismissed.

Paulo stared down at the dance floor for a full minute, filled with the distant thump of music. From her silence behind him, Paulo knew Alyssa was shocked, but she finally replied.

"Not quite done," she said, her voice shaking and thick. "Take your own advice. Let it go, already. Go see your brother. Accept the money from your father. Because the only one you're makin' suffer is yourself."

Paulo felt it all caving in on him again.

Then he heard the sound of the door opening, music spilling loudly into the room and then growing muffled with a click of the latch as it closed.

Alyssa was gone.

Anger bowled into him, returning with such a ferocious impact he had to move. He speared his fingers through his hair and turned to pace the floor. He'd been made the fool again.

Played.

He'd taken off for a few days to get his head on straight, and Alyssa had snuck off behind his back and gotten chummy with his ex-wife.

The turbulent emotion grew exponentially with every step. And he was glad he had stuck to his guns about the commitment. Because as he had stood at the bar, listening to her sabotage any hope of continuing their casual relationship, he'd been tempted to reconsider. And then came her announcement that she'd gone to see Bianca, was planning their *wedding* anniversary, and it had felt like a shotgun blast to the chest, knocking him back with a furious hit.

Footsteps ringing against the wood floor, he reached the wall and turned to keep going. He had been systematically stabbed in the back by every member of his family. His father. His brother. Even his wife. No way was he lining up for more.

He stopped pacing and braced an arm against the window, his mouth working, tightening his grip on the raging emotion.

There was no changing what had happened between them: Alyssa seeking out Bianca and choosing her version over his. Him striking back with his words.

Paulo balled his hand into a fist against the glass and stared, unseeing, down at the dance floor. He still couldn't believe what she'd done. Then again, it had taken him months to recover from Bianca's actions, too. His only solace this time was that the press wasn't involved.

Somehow the consolation didn't help one bit.

Paulo cut through the water, stretching his arms further, pumping his legs harder. His muscles screamed to take a rest. But each time he reached the end of his pool he flipped and kept going, his mind furiously at work.

Over a week had passed since the disaster at the club. And in that time Alyssa had been working from her apartment, while he spent every night at home, punishing himself in the water, both with hard exercise and by replaying their finale in his head.

He had yet to find a safe haven.

They had shared too much at the office. The track offered no relief. And his place was full of memories he'd be struggling to forget until the dawn of the next millennium. Everywhere he went he swore he smelled her perfume. In his living room. In his bedroom. Even on his bike.

There was no escape.

And every time the elusive lilac scent hit him, her absence made him ache, and he got angry all over again. But eventually that began to fade, and he couldn't even decide who he was mad at anymore. Alyssa, for hurting him? Or himself, for letting it happen? Finally he was left with nothing but this huge gaping hole. A void. And the silence no longer allowed him to ignore the word she'd used to describe him. The word that echoed relentlessly in his mind, even as he tried to push it away.

Cold.

If he hadn't known better, he would have thought she was talking about his father. The word described Ricardo Domingues to a T. Distant. Aloof. Paulo had never been able to figure out what made the man tick. Growing up, the only approved topic of conversation had been Domingues International. And while Marcos and his dad discussed business, Paulo had always felt left out. So he'd done what most kids would have done—sought the affections of his old man any way he could. But nothing had worked. When Paulo finished college, he joined him at the office, hoping he would finally be able to live up to the standard set by Marcos and earn his father's approval.

Pathetic. Pathetic and stupid.

Paulo reached the edge of the pool, executed a forward roll and pushed off, the hard kick of his legs propelled by his anger.

When he'd walked away from his father's business, he'd thought he was done. Was free of his family. He'd been proud of rising above the Domingues family trait of being defined by success. He scowled, water sleeking past his body, Alyssa's words ringing in his ears.

It had never occurred to him he was making the same mistake. That he was still letting his father influence him.

And this time it was his own damn fault.

Pain seared his thighs, enveloped his shoulders, but still he kept going. The repetitive slap of his arms and legs against the water was satisfying. And if Alyssa was right about his sorry excuse for a life, what else was she right about?

Something slapped the top of Paulo's head, and he stopped swimming. His T-shirt floated in the water, and he looked up to see Nick holding two beers in his left hand.

"Dude, as official best friend," Nick said as he approached, lit by pool lights, "I have to inform you that there *is* such a thing as too much exercise."

Paulo swam for the side and placed his elbows on the ledge, his chest heaving from exertion. "If you really cared about my health you'd be handing me a bottle of water, not a beer."

Nick shot him a mock shocked look. "They sell water in bottles?"

Despite his foul mood, Paulo let out a scoff of reluctant amusement.

Nick took a seat, dangling his legs in the pool, and handed Paulo his beer. They sat in silence as the water bucked and swayed from the aftermath of Paulo's strokes, pool lights flickering off the tile.

"I got an invitation to your brother's anniversary party." His friend paused, and the sound of lapping water filled the air. "It's this weekend."

Paulo set his bottle down with a clink. "I know when their anniversary is. I got an invitation, too." Raking a hand through his wet hair, he looked at Nick. "What is it you're really trying to say?"

It was the first time Paulo had seen his friend struck mute. But it didn't take long for Nick to recover.

"Okay…since you asked." Nick waved his hand to encompass the pool. "Is this your big plan? To hide out like a little girl because Alyssa said something you didn't want to hear?" He looked at him seriously. "Avoid her like you avoid your brother? Cuz I gotta tell you, bro. If it is—" he shook his head skeptically "—your plan reeks."

Paulo exhaled slowly through pursed lips. Nothing like the brutal honesty of an old friend. He picked up his beer and took a sip, the dark brew cooling his throat as he watched the pool light shimmy in the palm trees beyond the deck.

"What did Alyssa say to you, anyway?" Nick said.

"The abridged version?" Paulo gripped the hard glass in his hand and turned to look out into the dark beyond the trees. "That I'm an ass."

Nick chuckled. "Always knew she was a perceptive woman."

"Yeah," he said slowly. "That she is."

"So what's your next step?"

Paulo hesitated. He had spent hours pondering that question, and one thought refused to quit tailing him. No matter how hard he tried to shake it.

He wanted Alyssa. He wanted her in his life. But he couldn't make that happen without letting go of the last stronghold he'd been defending. Because the thought of taking a risk again always made his chest squeeze tight, constricting his lungs.

Scaring the hell out of him.

He shoved a hand through his hair and considered his choices. The tasks before him seemed insurmountable.

Alyssa's final words came back to him, and it seemed as good a place to start as any. "First, I'm going to go see my brother about the trust."

* * *

Located in downtown Miami, Domingues International headquarters dwarfed the surrounding buildings in both luxury and height, blocking the fierce noontime sun. Paulo parked in the circular drive and passed through the revolving glass door lined with gold paint.

Every muscle in Paulo's body grew heavy with memories as he rode the elevator to the suite that encompassed the top floor. His dad's old office.

Now it was his brother's.

Paulo exited the elevator and paused in a small alcove to look out the window, jamming his hands in his pockets. The view was one he would remember until the day he died. After every frustrating meeting with his father, Paulo would come to this spot, wondering if it was time to leave the company. Struggling between the need to stay and the desire to strike out on his own.

"What are you doing here?"

He turned and saw Marcos standing five feet away, wearing an impeccable suit and nothing short of a scowl on his face.

Hands planted on his hips, his brother said, "Did you come to give me more grief?"

Paulo supposed he deserved the terse greeting and unhappy expression. For a long time his own behavior had been fueled by anger. Anger was easier to handle, more familiar. Had become an old friend. And old friends were hard to say goodbye to.

"No, Marcos," Paulo finally said with resolve. "I'm done giving you grief. I only came to sign the trust papers." Another eternity passed as they stared at each other, and then, with no more than a curt nod, Marcos turned toward his office.

Paulo followed him into the spacious suite with its modern look that consisted of chrome, glass, sparse furniture and a bird's eye view of downtown. Marcos pulled a document from his desk and handed it to him. The thick legal file was heavy, and Paulo stared at it blankly.

The last legacy of his father.

He hadn't expected to do more than give a cursory signature to the papers and then leave the bloody building. There was nothing for him here. Certainly nothing worth reminiscing with his brother about. But when he saw his dad's familiar signature Paulo was hit with the irrepressible need to make sense of his father's actions—although he expected it was probably too late. The only man with the answers had been buried long ago.

Paulo tossed the file onto the glass top of Marcos's desk. "What did Dad expect to accomplish with this?" With a heavy sigh, he took a seat opposite his brother and flipped through the document, searching for the first line needing his signature. "That five years after his death he could make up for snubbing me in his will?"

"I never knew why Dad did anything that he did." Marcos sat in his leather chair across from Paulo. "And I was as surprised as you were when he left the entire company to me."

A harsh laugh rose from Paulo's throat as he wrestled with chronic, debilitating memories. "I don't know why. No matter how hard I worked, I could never compare to you." Not in school. Or later in college. And certainly not in the business—though he'd near killed himself trying. Jaw clenched, he reached for one of the pens perched in a silver cup, avoiding his brother's gaze. "Every time I accomplished something Dad would call me into his office—not to compliment me, but to compare my work to yours." Eyes fixed on the papers, he flipped through the document, not bothering to read as he scrawled his name in the marked spots. "And he made it plain that mine was never up to par."

"He did the same thing to me about you."

Shock reverberated through his body, and Paulo froze in the middle of his last signature, staggered by the news. Words failed him as he slowly looked up at his brother.

Marcos settled back in his seat, his stern face growing reflective. “Remember when I purchased the Hawthorne line of hotels? Dad had talked about the deal for two years, and I worked night and day to push the acquisition through. When I finally did…” He let out a forced breath, rubbing his chin. “The only thing he said to me was how the new boutique line *you* were proposing had more potential for growth.”

Pen clutched in his hand, the world as Paulo knew it took a decided tilt in a different direction, and then began to rotate in reverse. “You’re kidding me.”

“I wish I was,” his brother said, his expression harsh.

Struggling to reconcile the news with his memories, Paulo finished signing and closed the file, wishing that closing this chapter of his life could be accomplished as easily. As he tapped his pen on the desk, he gazed out over downtown Miami. “Why would he pit us against each other? It doesn’t make sense.”

Marcos said dryly, “Probably because he was a complete bastard.” The lines bracketing his mouth grew deeper. “But that could be my resentment talking.” He met Paulo’s gaze with a level one of his own. “Bianca would say it was to push us to achieve more. To train us for the cutthroat world of business.”

“You’ve discussed this with Bianca?”

“Of course I have. She’s my wife.”

The moment stretched tight, the tension so taut he could have bounced a quarter to the moon off the surface. All the things he’d wanted to say when his brother ran off with Bianca ran through his mind. The muscles in his jaw worked as he grappled for an appropriate response.

But he couldn’t find one.

After a long pause, his brother spared him the effort. “She didn’t leave you because of the money, Paulo,” Marcos said, his voice low. And, though Paulo’s first instinct was to reject the words, there was no lack of sincerity in his brother’s tone. “The reason she left was because she was afraid.”

Paulo cocked a disbelieving brow. "Afraid?"

"Yes," Marcos went on, his face set. "When her parents died she was barely out of high school, and she turned to Dad for support. She relied on him for everything."

Paulo shifted in his seat, uncomfortable with the direction of the conversation. "I know. Dad adored her."

"She adored him in return," Marcos said. "And when he had his stroke she was frightened. That was when she turned to me." With his pause, his eyes turned dark. "She had no one else to lean on. Because, even though she was married to you when Dad got sick—" he shot Paulo a hard look "—she was still very much alone."

Paulo slowly leaned back in his chair. Try as he might, other than a few cursory comments, Paulo couldn't remember discussing his father's illness with Bianca.

Not once.

But he remembered growing uncomfortable as she'd grown weepy during her attempts.

A wave of guilt slowly washed through him, and he tossed the pen to the desk with a grunt of self-disgust. He was the one to start asking the questions, but apparently there was no guarantee he would like the answers. It was time to own up to his role in the sordid mess that had been his marriage.

After wiping a weary hand down his face, Paulo finally responded. "Yeah." He dropped his hand to his lap. "I was a lousy excuse for a husband. Especially after Dad's stroke." His lips set, he shot his brother a rueful look. "I was too busy arguing with you about the business."

Marcos slowly nodded his head.

After a hard swallow, Paulo asked one final question. "So why did you two marry?"

Marcos hiked an eyebrow, as if the answer should be obvious. "We got married because we fell in love."

Paulo absorbed the blow, the blunt truth ricocheting, tearing holes in his long held beliefs.

Marcos went on. "Look, the months following Dad's stroke were chaotic. We were all under enormous stress." His shoulder rose and fell. "I can't say I handled it any better." He leaned his elbows on his desk, his fingers steepled together, studying Paulo over his hands. "But one thing I should have known was that your idea was never in danger of failing. Just like Dad, you've always been a shrewd businessman." Marcos stood and crossed to the plate glass overlooking downtown. "I should have listened to you about starting the new line," he said, staring out the window. "Maybe Dad knew you were better off running your own show." Finally, he turned and fixed a steady gaze on Paulo. "It could be he left the company to me as a way of forcing you to take that step."

Pursing his lips, Paulo considered the scenario. The concept was difficult to buy, but certainly within the realm of possibility. And, after all he'd just learned, someone could accuse his dad of being a foreign spy and Paulo would believe them.

"Maybe he did." Paulo sent his brother a dry smile. "Or maybe he *was* just a bastard, through and through." Marcos let out an amused scoff, and Paulo shrugged in resignation. "Either way, we'll never know."

And, while the overdue conversation with his brother had come with several surprising revelations, Paulo was only sure about one thing...he didn't care anymore.

Marcos crossed back to his desk and leaned his hands on the surface, looking at him intently. "We could merge the two companies."

Paulo watched his brother, the offer hanging between them. But as far as his business was concerned he had everything he needed. And he was right where he wanted to be.

In the driver's seat.

"Thanks for the offer," Paulo said as he stood. With a wry

grin, he stuck out his hand. "Why don't we just figure out how to be brothers?"

Marcos let out a small laugh, his face relaxing as he returned his handshake.

Paulo's grin grew bigger. "I don't do partners so well."

As soon as the words left his lips, his thoughts turned to the one person he *did* team well with. Alyssa had felt like a partner in every sense of the word. At work. At play. And in bed. The longing to see her again was fierce, and brought a sucker punch to his stomach.

As Paulo headed for the exit, he was keenly aware of the huge, yawning space left by the one woman who had taken a piece of him when she'd left. Now that he'd completed the first task he'd formulated after his swim, he was at a loss over how to approach the second—and much more important—of the two.

How the hell was he going to make things right with Alyssa?

CHAPTER ELEVEN

IT WAS late when Alyssa entered her apartment with her shopping bags, disappointed her mom's retail intervention had failed. When her mother had stopped by and seen the state Alyssa was in, she'd given her a hug and dragged her out of the house. But after two weeks of crying, moping, working, and working some more, nothing could wipe away, even briefly, the vision of Paulo's back as he had dismissed her at the club.

As she placed her bags on the sofa she heard the sound of Paulo's voice on her answering machine, asking her to pick up the phone, and her footsteps faltered. A wave of longing hit—so strong she pressed a hand to her chest.

She missed Paulo. Her heart ached for him. His sense of humor. The way he made her feel. Real. Free. And alive.

Gloriously, gloriously alive.

Entering the dining room, she listened, slowly sinking into a chair as he gave up asking her to pick up and went on. His voice was serious, the volume low as he spoke. "There's something we have to discuss." Her throat closed over and her heart expanded until it felt too big for her chest. She'd been waiting two miserably endless weeks for some sign of a breakthrough, and she prayed this was it.

Paulo went on. "I'm afraid the success at the hotel has made you worthy of gossiping newspapers. I don't know if you've seen today's *Miami Insider*, but I wanted to warn you. There's a small blip detailing your criminal record." Numb, Alyssa listened to him let out a sigh, sounding frustrated as he continued, "We can discuss it at my brother's anniversary party tomorrow."

The click of the phone disconnecting was loud, and pain flashed bright, hot. And—just like a laser beam—it cleanly separated her heart into two. Neatly cauterizing the edges. No hope for healing remained. After treating her so coldly, there still had been no apology. Worse, Paulo hadn't even called to talk about the two of them.

He'd only called to warn her the past had caught up with her.

Motionless, she stared at the answering machine. Right now, countless Miamians were reading about her shady history. She should feel…something. Humiliation? Defeat? Yet nothing.

All she felt was a crushing sadness. After days of hoping Paulo would finally come through, it was time to admit their relationship was circling the dead-end cul-de-sac of his heart. There was nowhere to go. No matter how stubborn she was, she had to face the fact that the man she loved couldn't love her back.

Sagging against the table, she covered her face with her hands. He'd warned her from the start he was unavailable, but she hadn't listened. And now he was going to pay the price for her mistake. Because who would want to schedule their precious functions at the Samba with a known criminal as its event planner?

The lonely silence grew as she dropped her hands and looked around her dining room. Her phone sat on the table next to the invitation to Bianca's anniversary party. In lieu of a cupboard, several filing cabinets lined the wall, containing all the information she'd gathered over the years. Vendors, contacts, events she'd organized. Her gaze landed on the newspaper article about the reception at the Samba, now hanging on her wall. Everything that used to be important.

But what she wanted had changed.

Paulo was right: she'd paid her debt to society. She deserved to be happy. To pursue her dreams. She exhaled slowly, combing shaky fingers through her hair. But she had to quit her job at the Samba. Because, no matter how much he'd hurt her with his words at the club, the consequences of the article should be hers and hers alone.

She sat up and reached for the anniversary invitation on her dining room table. She hadn't planned on going. And after the tabloid article about her it would be best if she stayed far, far away. But she refused to cower like a mangy dog anymore. Plus, she had to put things right for Paulo.

The Samba was important to him, and she couldn't let the man she loved suffer because of her.

Alyssa concentrated on keeping her breathing easy as she stood in the doorway to the country club ballroom. Casino tables and roulette wheels circled the dance floor. While dealers shuffled cards and took bets, a small jazz band played in the corner. The sound of poker chips and laughter rang in the room as guests in cocktail dresses and suits milled about. She'd passed the Ducati on the way in, which meant Paulo was here.

Perspiration dotted her lip, and Alyssa ran a hand down the crepe jacket of her designer pantsuit, focusing on the texture. It was airy. Pretty, yet casual. And blessedly comfortable.

You look great, Alyssa. Now go in there and get this done.

After squaring her shoulders, she made her way through the crowd and, with no idea where Paulo was, randomly headed for the roulette wheel. As she passed the blackjack table she spied Tessa Harrison. For a moment their gazes locked, and the stunned expression above the lady's hand of cards was almost funny.

But Alyssa just ignored her and kept walking, too distracted by queasiness to give the woman much thought. The bumbling butterflies dancing in her belly were getting pretty rowdy.

Because giving Paulo up, even if all they had left was a work relationship, was going to be tough. She'd never see him again.

Her heart crumpled at the thought, and she stumbled slightly in her casual high-heeled sandals.

"I was hoping to see you here," Paulo said from behind.

She cringed and came to a halt, bracing for the hurdle she had to clear. The one she wasn't ready for. The one she would never be ready for. Slowly, she turned to face him.

He was wearing a tuxedo, black hair trimmed but still long enough to keep the roguish look. And the mocha cappuccino gaze was the same. He looked too gorgeous for words. A tinge of unwanted desire slipped out before she could contain it.

His level gaze was guarded. "After the article, I wasn't sure you would come."

She fingered the edge of her jacket, hoping to soothe her frayed nerves. But she had a job to do. And, come hell or high tide, no matter how difficult, she was going to do it. "I've never run away from anything in my life," she said. "And I certainly don't intend to start now."

"You ran from my bed that first morning."

She blinked, searching for a response. "I was just postponing the inevitable."

"And the second morning?"

Frowning, she tensed her forehead. "I had work to do."

"Convenient, all these excuses," he said as he stepped closer.

The deep voice and his proximity had the butterflies in her belly shifting from the Texas Two-step to thumping hip-hop. She turned to look out the window overlooking the bay, collecting herself before meeting his gaze again.

"We have a few things to discuss," he said with a determined tone. "But why don't we start with a dance?"

Heart beating furiously, she gripped the strap of her purse. She couldn't get sidetracked by how good he looked, or how wonderful it would feel to be in his arms. And putting this off wasn't going to make it any easier. "The time for dancing has ended, Paulo." She swallowed against the lump in her throat. "I'm moving out of the Samba. I'm going to rent office space for Elite Events."

His brows pinched together in doubt.

"I'm going to tell Charles to hire an assistant," she continued. "Someone who can help coordinate things while he looks for another event planner." Alyssa cleared her throat, trying to loosen the tight muscles, but it was hard to keep her voice even. "I'm not renewing our contract."

A dark look flickered in Paulo's eyes. "Why?"

She stared up at him, torn by the answer to his question.

Shifting even closer, Paulo looked down on her. "You keep saying you don't run. So what does this qualify as?" His stare was intense. "A fast walk in the opposite direction?"

Was he really trying to convince her to stay? Her work wasn't that important. She could be replaced. And hadn't he thought about what the newspaper article would mean? "It qualifies as me trying to do the right thing," she said. "My past is now widely known in Miami."

A furrow of disgust appeared on his brow. "That sleazy newspaper is a worthless piece of scum."

Dear God, was he *trying* to make this more difficult for her? With her fist clenched, she tried again. "It could affect business at the Samba."

"I doubt that. And it doesn't matter if it does."

She pressed her hand to her temple, forcing herself to go on. And this time she included a part of the truth. "I can't have you paying the price for my sins."

"To hell with the article. You've paid the price already. You shouldn't have to keep on paying."

She closed her lids, cutting off the vision of Paulo. The sound of the roulette wheel clicked in the background as conversation lagged. She hated how weak he made her feel. Hated how a few little words could sap her resolve to let him go.

But just because he'd come to Bianca and Marcos's party, just because he was a man of principle who believed she'd paid her dues, was willing to brave the effects of bad publicity, it didn't mean anything had changed. The rest was nice, but there were bigger issues at hand. Like the fact she loved him. And he couldn't love her back.

She opened her eyes. "I can't work with you anymore," she said, and turned to walk away.

He grabbed her hand. "Don't go." His fingers firmly held her in place while his eyes searched hers, and then he shoved both hands in his pockets, staring at her as he shuffled his feet. An odd anticipation settled in her gut. She'd never seen Paulo nervous.

"I have something to give you," he said.

Her gaze dropped to his tuxedo pocket. His fist was bunched, as if curled around an object. And, despite all the fresh air circling around them, Alyssa couldn't find enough oxygen. Because with absolute certainty she knew Paulo had a ring in his pocket. Her heart lost speed, its rate barely able to supply blood to her brain, and time lapsed into slow motion.

Without saying a word, without so much as a peep of explanation, he began to kneel down, and Alyssa's heart stalled completely.

Her lids stretched wide. That was it? She blinked. No discussion needed? The rushing rise of emotion blasted through her body, her thoughts swirling. Because popping the question and giving her a ring didn't necessarily signify he was ready for an honest relationship.

He had put a ring on a woman's finger before and it had meant nothing.

The pain she'd felt each time he froze her out came roaring back, and she dragged in a breath, her chest hurting. She needed him so much, and the thought of being married to Paulo, waiting for him to participate, was too painful to contemplate. Waiting…like Bianca had.

She couldn't live like that. Which meant she had to refuse his offer.

His knee landed on the floor, and her thoughts raced. He'd chased her so hard. Dragged her out into the sunshine to breathe the fresh air of a life beyond work. To feel. To want. To *love*. And along the way he'd annihilated every ounce of her reserve.

As he began to pull his hand from his pocket, her legs turned to jelly.

She couldn't do it. She wouldn't be strong enough to say no.

When he flipped open the box without a single word panic seized her, and she pivoted on her heel, blindly pushing her way into the crowd.

Paulo stared, dumbfounded, at the sight of Alyssa disappearing into the small mob that had gathered around them curiously.

She was leaving.

The granite floor was hard against his knee. The collective held breath of the crowd around him was strained. But every cell in his body was too stupefied to move.

Alyssa was walking away. With his intentions so clearly stamped in his posture, she was leaving him. But it wasn't as if he hadn't been through this before. This feeling of desertion. Some of it was deserved, like Bianca. Some of it wasn't, such as his father. His brother was a bit of both. But every single incident—every one of them—had hurt.

But *nothing* compared to the excruciating pain of watching Alyssa walk away.

He closed his eyes, clamping the jewelry box shut. The crowd began to murmur and shift, flowing around him, resuming their activities. But Paulo couldn't move.

When he'd read that blasted article in the paper, his first instinct—right after squashing the need to tear the journalist apart—had been to fix the problem. Make it go away for her. But it was a done deal. There was no undoing the damage.

And then all he'd wanted was to find her and pull her into his arms. To protect her. But, because of his dumb actions, he didn't have that right. And he *wanted* the privilege of being the one to take on the world for her. He'd thought he could make this easier by skipping past all the awkward parts and going straight to what he wanted…a life with Alyssa.

Truly, he was the King of Stupid.

He opened his eyes and stared in the direction of the exit. He should chase her down. Talk to her. Try to convince her to change her mind.

Frowning, he lowered his hand to his knee. Or maybe he'd hurt her so much that she couldn't forgive his asinine behavior. And what if he let go, cracked his chest open and let it all spill out, only to have her refuse his proposal again?

How would he recover?

With a scowl, Paulo slammed the door on the cowardly thought and stood up. Alyssa had faced down her fears so many times, in so many ways, it defied comprehension. Yet he didn't have the guts to do it once.

Not *once*.

And if he didn't have the courage to go after her, he didn't deserve her. If he didn't go after her *now*, she'd be lost to him forever. Her smile, her spunk, her cool wit and their combustible passion relegated to a distant memory—until he grew so old and bitter he wouldn't be able to stand being on the same continent with himself.

Paulo shoved the ring in his pocket and took off toward the exit.

She didn't have time to call for a taxi. Hoping to hail one from the street, Alyssa hurried up the country club driveway, her steps faltering when she heard a shout from behind. Her heart constricted, stealing her breath.

Paulo.

Moving quickly, she rounded the gate and dashed across the northbound lane, the cars held back by a red light. When she landed on the palm-tree-lined median, her heels sank into the grass. She glanced back and saw Paulo approaching. With her teeth clamped on her lip, she turned to stare at the cars whipping by between her and the sidewalk on the other side. Maybe she should take her chances. Just dart across and hope her timing worked out.

Good grief. She was desperate, but she wasn't crazy. Her chest heaved as she blew out a sigh. And if Paulo was ready to talk, ready to have a *real* heart-to-heart, this was as good a place as any.

Mentally preparing for battle, she turned to watch him wait for a break in the streaming line of vehicles freed by the traffic signal. She'd had a moment to collect herself. To push aside her hurt. And that made way for the other growing emotion.

Anger was now riding shotgun with her pain.

When the line of cars stretched far enough apart, he jogged across the lane and came to a stop in front of her. "That absolutely qualified as running away."

The words smashed the last of her restraint. "No." She tried to stomp her foot, but her heel caught in the ground. Frustrated, she went on. "That was me refusing a proposal that was nothing more than an empty romantic gesture. And I'm not the one who's running." She finally wrenched her shoe free. "You are!"

"Alyssa—"

"You think you can just show up and offer me a ring in front of a crowd?" she said, her drawling words loud. "As if whippin' out a piece of jewelry suddenly makes everything okay?" Her nails dug into her palms, and she forced herself to slow her words. "I don't want you down on your knee. I don't want a public proposal." She stepped closer, looking up at him. "I want *honesty*."

He crossed his arms, his tuxedo jacket drawing tight on his broad shoulders. "You want honesty? How about this? It's hell watching your wife walk away, even if it's mostly your fault." Shocked by his admission, she was struck mute. The pause stretched, traffic now whizzing by on both sides. "And up until now there was no way I was going to put myself through that possibility again."

She couldn't belittle his fears, but she also couldn't ignore her own. "She left because of the way you treated her."

He didn't bother to deny it. "Yes."

"So how do I know this time will be different?"

He sighed and raked his hair from his forehead. "To start with, for once I'm actually in love."

Her heart soared, but her head pounded, keeping her focused. "That's wonderful. But let me tell you something. If you don't have the actions to back it up, it won't be enough." Feeling surer of her argument, she tipped her chin, her voice stronger. "And you know what? You were right. I *do* deserve a life. And I'm not going to settle for less anymore. So if you want me, than you have to put yourself out there. *Really* take a risk. Because if you can't—" She blinked back the stinging threat of tears. "If you can't, we don't stand a chance."

"I don't know where to start."

"Start with telling me what you want."

After a pause, Paulo held out his hand, the velvet box in his palm. "I want you," he said as he flipped open the lid. "Marry me."

A large diamond solitaire sparkled in the sun, and the pounding in her temples spread to her chest as she stared at it. Everything she wanted was right there in front of her. Unfortunately she hadn't heard all she needed to hear.

A semi-truck swooshed by, kicking up a diesel-scented gust

of air that blew her hair across her eyes. Blinking, she swiped away the strands, her hand shaking. But she remained silent.

With an apprehensive expression, he glanced around and then turned his gaze back to scan hers. “Is this not unromantic enough for you?”

“It’s not about the location. It’s about your words.”

After a brief hesitation, ring still displayed in his hand, he said quietly, “You’re not going to make this easy, are you?”

“Life isn’t easy. Marriage won’t always be easy.” She glanced down at the ring and back to his beautiful face, gathering her strength to press on. There was no other choice. “You have to convince me this time around will be different.”

His chest rose and fell on a huge breath. “Okay.” With a determined look, he stepped closer, his voice burning with the same intensity reflected in his eyes. “From the first moment you showed up at my hotel, sassing me by the pool, I’ve wanted you. I kept telling myself it was a temporary fling.” He frowned, looking down on her. “But I couldn’t let you go.”

“Maybe that was just the sex.”

“It was more than just sex.” He paused and shook his head. “But I was too dense to recognize it. And then you faced me down and sided with Bianca, and it was too painful to deal with.”

“I sided with the *truth*.”

He placed his fingers on her mouth, and her body instantly began to purr. She fought the urge to lean closer.

“I know that.” His eyes grew gentle, followed by his tone. “At least I do now.” His lips tipped up into that killer half-smile. “And a heartfelt confession strong enough to make up for some serious sins is hard to pull off when I keep getting interrupted.” He dropped his hand, and instantly her lips felt lonely.

She swallowed, her throat burning with emotion. “I’ll shut up.”

“Just until I finish.” He cupped her jaw with his free hand

and shifted closer, until they were toe to toe, the offered ring still between them. "I've never been in love before, Alyssa." His face was tight, a hint of fear beneath the sincerity. Her vision blurred, and she blinked hard at the tears as he continued. "Didn't *want* to be in love. After my experience with family, all the rejection, I figured life was easier that way. Because after a while…" A flicker of raw pain crossed his face, cutting her deep. "A guy starts to wonder if there isn't something inherently wrong with *him*."

The sheen of tears finally breached her lashes, and her vision cleared as they slipped down her cheeks. The cocky charmer, full of self-doubt? Who would have guessed?

"Can I say something now?" she asked.

He rubbed the wet track on her face with his thumb. "Only if it's something I want to hear."

She laid a loving palm on his cheek, her voice full of conviction. "There is nothing wrong with you." With a small sniff and a wobbly smile, she amended her statement. "At least nothing that a swift kick in the ass won't fix."

He chuckled softly. But as the amusement died away he grew serious again, his eyes searching hers. "I want to believe that. But I'm still scared senseless that you'll discover you were wrong about me and take off. It's a scary thought." He sent her a look that was breathtakingly frank. "But nowhere near as scary as living the rest of my life without you." Paulo glanced down at the ring he still held between them. "My arm is getting tired," he said, and a flicker of panic crossed his face. "Please tell me you'll marry me."

She laid her palm on the box. "I'll marry you."

His fingers closed around her hand and he let out a sigh of relief, leaning his forehead against hers. His voice was rough, his hazel gaze glowing. "Now tell me you love me."

Alyssa looked up at him, letting it all shine in her eyes. "I love you."

His mouth closed over hers. With a tiny squeak of relief, she reached up with her free hand and gripped his lapel, pulling him closer. Paulo's lips grew more insistent, and she savored the taste of him. The hard chest beneath her fingers.

A few discordant honks peppered the air, and a wolf whistle from a passing motorist had Alyssa pulling away. With shaking fingers, she smoothed the wrinkles she'd left on his jacket.

Paulo smiled as he stepped back, holding out his arms. "You never told me what you thought of my tuxedo."

An unfamiliar feeling of joy bubbled up in her heart. "It will be perfect for our wedding."

He shot her a suspiciously winning grin. "Hmm," he said as he dropped his hands to her hips. "Now that we're engaged, are you going to tell me how you got that file?"

Raising her eyebrows, she struggled to maintain a deadpan face. "It will be my gift to you on our fiftieth wedding anniversary."

The mischievous spark in his eyes grew brighter, and he pulled her against him. It was like coming home. His voice went low, seductive. "Make it the twenty-fifth, and I guarantee it'll be worth your efforts."

Alyssa finally let out a laugh, giddy with happiness. "It's a deal."

"Do I still get to keep you as my strategic partner?"

"Of course," Alyssa said, sending him a smile that must rival the blazing sun above. "But you, Mr. Domingues, now hold the permanent number one position on my to-do list."

* * * * *

New York Times and *USA TODAY* bestselling author
Maya Banks presents book three in her miniseries
PREGNANCY & PASSION.

TEMPTED BY HER INNOCENT KISS

Available March 2012 from Harlequin Desire!

There came a time in a man's life when he knew he was well and truly caught. Devon Carter stared down at the diamond ring nestled in velvet and acknowledged that this was one such time. He snapped the lid closed and shoved the box into the breast pocket of his suit.

He had two choices. He could marry Ashley Copeland and fulfill his goal of merging his company with Copeland Hotels, thus creating the largest, most exclusive line of resorts in the world, or he could refuse and lose it all.

Put in that light, there wasn't much he could do except pop the question.

The doorman to his Manhattan high-rise apartment hurried to open the door as Devon strode toward the street. He took a deep breath before ducking into his car, and the driver pulled into traffic.

Tonight was the night. All of his careful wooing, the countless dinners, kisses that started brief and casual and became more breathless—all a lead-up to tonight. Tonight his seduction of Ashley Copeland would be complete, and then he'd ask her to marry him.

He shook his head as the absurdity of the situation hit him for the hundredth time. Personally, he thought William Copeland was crazy for forcing his daughter down Devon's throat.

Ashley was a sweet enough girl, but Devon had no desire

HDEXP0312

to marry anyone.

William had other plans. He'd told Devon that Ashley had no head for the family business. She was too softhearted, too naive. So he'd made Ashley part of the deal. The catch? Ashley wasn't to know of it. Which meant Devon was stuck playing stupid games.

Ashley was supposed to think this was a grand love match. She was a starry-eyed woman who preferred her animal-rescue foundation over board meetings, charts and financials for Copeland Hotels.

If she ever found out the truth, she wouldn't take it well.

And hell, he couldn't blame her.

But no matter the reason for his proposal, before the night was over, she'd have no doubts that she belonged to him.

What will happen when Devon marries Ashley?
Find out in Maya Banks's passionate new novel
TEMPTED BY HER INNOCENT KISS
Available March 2012 from Harlequin Desire!

HDEXP0312